Holding on to a Sound Mind

Holding on to a Sound Mind

Ann Elizabeth Yeager

ISBN-13: 978-1-7339583-0-1

First Printing: September, 2019

About the Cover: Katy Huggins designed the cover of this novel. She lives in Pearland, TX.

Printed in the United States

For Mom and Pop,
my best cheerleaders

Contents

Introduction

I spent six months of 2012-2013 in a group home, and the experience changed my life. The time at the group home was not easy, but the experience helped me to see what I needed to do to be a more stable person. While I lived in the home, I attended an outpatient program for people with mental health issues. Before attending the outpatient program, I spent twenty-eight days in an inpatient treatment facility to recover from a mental breakdown. While in inpatient and outpatient services, I learned many coping skills that I felt were crucial to my survival, things that helped me to "hold on to a sound mind," hence the title. I also learned to depend on God more, to really seek Him; and He strengthened my faith. After my group home stay, I decided to write a fictionalized account about a young woman recovering from a bout with her mental illness who applied these coping skills and the reality of her faith to her life.

Some people may think that this book is written like a memoir. Perhaps this notion may exist because I used a good bit of my own story and background in the book. The protagonist is based on my personhood, but I mixed truth and fiction in a way that I hope is a good attempt at a realistic fictional novel. I changed some characters, details, conversations and situations in the story. The protagonist is also a much younger version of me. Thus, this book is inspired by a true story, but it is fiction at the same time.

If this book can impact a society bent on prejudice and bigotry against people with mental illness, help diffuse the

stigma of mental illness in our communities, help those
with mental health issues, and educate those who know of
a relative or friend who struggle with their mental health,
then I will have accomplished my purpose for this book. I
certainly hope you enjoy it.

1

The Main Hospital

RIGHT ABOUT THE TIME of dawn, the hoarse, loud, desperate strain in a woman's voice echoed throughout the halls of the mental hospital. Her voice became louder, and she sounded more terrified with each moment that passed. She was yelling at the psych techs.

"Leave me alone! This ain't real! This ain't real!" she cried.

She was right outside Hannah's room door, next to the group table. Hannah could hear the woman scattering pencils and crayons across the floor, destroying the group board games, hollering to no one and everyone at the same time. Of course, no one on that wing was still asleep. The ruckus between the hysterical woman and the psych techs trying to calm her ruined all possibility of a smooth transition into the morning. Hannah Truefield, a psych-iatric patient, was glad she might be going home soon. These periodic early morning fits from new intakes grew more disconcerting as the days passed.

Hannah could hear the psych techs trying to calm the woman down.

"Okay. We're not going to hurt you. I'm just going to hold your legs," said a psych tech.

"Leave me alone!" cried the woman.

Another psych tech spoke loudly. "I'm going to hold you under your arms, and we're going to carry you out, okay? It's going to be okay."

"This ain't right! This ain't right!" cried the woman.

Hannah could hear them carry her out the doors of the wing with the woman hollering all the way out. Hannah listened for any more commotion and only heard the doors slamming shut. Then, silence filled the wing of the hospital. She got up and went to the bathroom. Hannah was a young woman with auburn red curls and a heavyset physique. She had a square jaw, a crooked smile, and hazel-green eyes. She splashed cold water on her face, brushed her teeth, and fluffed out her hair. Then she changed out of her pajamas into day clothes and walked out of her room to line up for breakfast. Her mind was foggy from just waking up from the heavy cocktail of medicine she had taken the night before.

As the psych tech in charge gave the breakfast call, sleepy-eyed patients began to come out of their rooms in slow motion. Morning was always rough for patients with a mental illness—it meant they had to face another day, another potentially difficult day. They awoke from a sedated sleep into the uncomfortable reality that they were still sick and in the hospital for it. As they trudged into the elevator which took them downstairs, they eventually reached the outside walkway and entered the cafeteria.

As Hannah followed the line into the dining hall, she periodically checked her back, a practice she adopted in the hospital, where her stay felt more like being in jail than being in a mental ward. She was wary of the other patients, and Hannah trusted only her doctor.

As Hannah ate her eggs and toast, she kept her eyes down and focused on her meal. Out of all of their activities, she hated mealtime the worst. She was overstimulated by the noise in the large hall, and some patient sitting near her always managed to talk obnoxiously loud. After she finished her meal, Hannah would sit at the dinner table, plug her ears with her index fingers, close her eyes, and breathe deeply. She was trying to endure the wait before the techs escorted the patients outside for a while.

Going outside was a relief. Most of the patients took a smoke break on the smoker's patio, a lifted deck of wood and benches designated for smokers only. The rest of the patients either took a walk around the quadrangle at the center of the campus or stood near the entrance to the building, waiting to go back inside. Hannah walked by herself along the covered sidewalk that surrounded the quadrangle. She breathed deep and inhaled the cool December air. Today was an important day. She knew her doctor was possibly going to discharge her. She just might be getting out.

After being outside for about twenty minutes, the techs brought all the patients on Hannah's wing back inside. Hannah felt more awake now. Her stomach full, her body more relaxed after the unpleasant wakening, Hannah walked to the door of her doctor's office and sat in a waiting chair next to the door. When it was time to see the doctor, Hannah walked in and took a seat, and her doctor's eyes met hers. Dr. Mitchell was wearing a white lab coat and preppy glasses. Her greyish blonde hair was pulled back in a neat ponytail.

"Hello, Hannah," said her doctor gently.

Hannah's deep hazel-green eyes showed the strain of a psychological workout.

"Hi," she replied softly, sighing deeply.

Sitting in the sterile, cramped, dingy office, Hannah waited as her doctor peered over her reading glasses and looked seriously into Hannah's eyes. For the past month, Hannah had seen her faithful, patient doctor every day. Dr. Mitchell had been treating her for several years. She was a loyal, deeply devoted physician who understood well the horrible effects that mental illness can prevail upon a person.

"So, you ready to take the leap?" asked Dr. Mitchell.

"I guess so," quivered Hannah, feeling unsure and insecure.

"I know you've been through this before, but you need to remember that people with your disorder find acclimating back into society very difficult."

Hannah nodded and smiled weakly, taking in the warning while carrying the tremendous weight of antici-pation on her shoulders. Thinking deeply, she brushed her bob of natural curls out of her face and sighed. What she wanted most was to maintain her sanity and eventually secure independence. She wanted to live on her own. Autonomy. Self-sufficiency. Was that possible? She determined to set high standards and shoot for the sky when she focused on her aspirations. Sanity and independence were her continual goals.

"Are you sure the group home is my only option?"

"You have to make that decision," said her doctor.

"Do you think you could live in an apartment right now?"

Hannah thought for a moment. She couldn't even figure out how to use the outside line for the phone at the hospital. How could she possibly live on her own? She was not ready to leave the main hospital, but she did not want to stay either. It was time for her to go. After 28 days of inpatient psychiatric hospitalization, Hannah realized that she was about to enter a world she had never known—life in a group home. In the hospital, she had followed all the rules of grueling inpatient treatment. She woke up early, got herself ready, went to all the group meetings during the day, walked with the other residents to every meal, took her medicine regularly, and took her showers at night. Now, she wanted the reward of independence, just like the rest of the patients surrounding her, but could she really handle the responsibility that comes with freedom?

She had conceded only in the last few days that she was willing to go into a group home. Her parents were unable to care for her in her precarious condition as she made the transition back into functioning reality. Hannah was in her late twenties and had been a surprise birth for her older parents. Her mom was thirty-three when she was born; her dad was thirty-nine. Hannah was the baby of three. Her parents took care of her earlier in her illness years ago but couldn't make that commitment now. Her dad showed early onset Parkinson's, and her mom needed to take care of him.

"Please just let me come home," Hannah had begged.

"Darling, we can't take care of you. I need to look after your daddy. I'm sorry."

Hannah couldn't ask her parents to take on the monumental assignment of helping her recover from a mental breakdown. Given her dad's illness, Hannah just couldn't be with them this time. She was on her own, diving into the pool of uncertainty with an unsteadiness that made her fall upon everything they taught her in the main hospital— all the coping skills needed to handle the scariness of stress that once led to her mental demise.

The main coping skill she had learned while in the inpatient hospital was meditation. She would focus on a peaceful scene and hold the visual in her mind and meditate on it. The process kept her calm and able to endure stressful situations. Another coping skill was practicing breathing techniques. She would inhale and hold her breath for just so long. Then she would exhale and inhale again and hold it for longer than before. Finally, her last inhaled breath would come, and she would hold it in even longer, for as long as she could, then exhale. The process helped to relax her, and the skill was invaluable to her.

In the doctor's office, Hannah breathed deeply as she thought of everything she endured in less than a month—

confusion, irritability, unrest, agitation, and endless anxiety—in short, a living nightmare. With the order official from Dr. Mitchell that Hannah would be discharged that day, she thanked her doctor and stood up, her shoulders slumped in a depressed state, her body weakened by lack of sleep. She had only recently started sleeping at night, and the extended insomnia with which she faced for most of her stay there took its toll on her. From looking at her, with her body clothed in a baggy, gray sweatsuit, one would never have known she was once a competitive athlete. She dragged her weary body toward her hospital room.

"Strip your bed," said a psych tech.

Hannah nodded and walked back into the room that had been her home for the past month. As she pulled the plain linens off her bed, she thought about her experience in the inpatient hospital. The ritualistic routine of her days was merciless. Never allowed to be alone for very long, Hannah attended difficult group therapy sessions where the obnoxious vented and the introverts tried not to fall asleep. Most of the time, the group therapist on the wing that day had a way of making the patients feel safe in a seemingly unsafe environment. She did expect them to stay in group for the forty-five-minute duration.

"Today our topic is mindfulness or being present with your thoughts in the moment as they happen," said the therapist on a particularly hot and humid fall afternoon.

Hannah struggled to practice this suggested mindfulness as she tried to sustain rational thoughts in a brain under great duress. She had sustained a barrage of voices in her head for about three weeks out of the month that she was in the main hospital—oppressive voices who cursed at her, contradicted her, and waylaid her self-esteem. She tried both ignoring the voices and arguing with them. Sometimes she heard specific commands. Sometimes she heard insults. The voices persisted in tormenting her until she almost didn't return to sanity. A miracle drug was the only thing that could bring her back to reality. Her doctor happened to know of one, and a special medication rescued Hannah from the grips of a mental onslaught.

SITTING AT THE GROUP TABLE in the hospital wing, Hannah anxiously clutched her garbage bag full of all her possessions and stared at a page in a magazine. She wore the outfit she had worn when she came into the inpatient hospital—black dress pants, a dressy blouse, and black boots. Hannah didn't wear a belt because they weren't allowed on the hospital wing, so keeping her pants up was a challenge. She sat at a table next to the nurse's station, waiting to be escorted to her next destination.

Amy, her favorite psych tech, approached her. She was a kind woman with good people skills.

"You did good," said Amy. "You did everything you were supposed to do—you came to group, you did what was asked of you, you took your medicine. That's real good, girl."

Hannah smiled and shook Amy's hand, the first act of physical expression that Hannah ever initiated while she was in the main hospital. Since Hannah was leaving, she felt it was appropriate to make the physical contact to show her appreciation for such a wonderful staffer. Hannah promised herself that she would hold Amy in her heart as an example of lovingkindness, a treasured trait to come across in a mental hospital, where such goodness sometimes gets hidden behind sterile professionalism.

"I want to show you something, girl," said Amy. Hannah followed her into the empty group therapy room where one wall was completely covered in windows, showing a view outside.

"You see that tree, Hannah?" asked Amy, pointing outside to a small oak. Hannah looked at the tree.

"See how that wind blows those leaves and bends those branches? That little tree is just doggone determined not to move from where he's supposed to be. You know why? He's hanging on to his roots. They go deep down in the soil. No way he can move with all them roots holding him steady. That's why the wind can't blow him away. When you go on the outside and get where you're supposed to be, you're going to face a lot of wind, Hannah. Sometimes that wind is going to blow you so hard, you may feel like you're just going to blow away. But you just hang on to your roots, and you'll be okay. Okay, Hannah?"

Hannah smiled and nodded. "Okay, Amy," she said.

Hannah walked back into the main area and sat at the table, next to her belongings. Her caseworker, Sylvia, came to talk to her. A tall, slender, attractive woman, she spoke to Hannah in a gentle voice.

"We have you scheduled to go to your group home today. You can take the group home van at outpatient at three o'clock, and you can move in then," she said.

"Thank you," said Hannah.

Grant, an older, stocky man, wheeled in a dolly to carry Hannah's possessions—three changes of clothing, her Bible and prayer book, numerous papers she collected from group, and toiletries. A white plastic bag held the large number of goods in a pitiful, sagging state. She was now officially a bag lady.

As Grant escorted her off the wing, she waved goodbye to the nursing staff. Grant and Hannah quietly rode down the elevator, and he led her outside past the smokers' patio and onto the main walkway. Hannah and Grant didn't speak, and she recognized the need to be silent at a time like this one. She took determined, long steps, taking in the quiet and the weight of her experience there in the inpatient hospital.

She had once walked on that same walkway as a distant, confused, troubled woman. Now, she held strides as a seasoned veteran who had endured an immensely challenging, psychological boot camp. She held her shoulders back with hope. If she thought about her future, she would give in to fear, so she was only mindful of the present.

Grant led Hannah through the door that led to the main hospital's entrance, and she waited on Grant to talk to a supervisor in the business office. Standing there, waiting to be fully released, Hannah noticed a print on the wall. The picture was *Iris Garden*, by Vincent van Gogh, her most favorite artist. Hannah gazed upon the artwork and felt a connection to the troubled Van Gogh who had experienced time in an asylum just like she had.

Her final goodbye took place just inside the lobby of the entrance to the main hospital.

"Thanks. God bless," she said to Grant as she gave him a hug—something that would never have happened inside the hospital wing.

"You too," he answered.

As he walked away, leaving her bag of clothes with her, she felt a strange uneasiness about what she was supposed to do now. Her orders from the nurse were to meet with a van in outpatient services that would bring her to her new temporary home—the group home. She maintained a sense of composure by focusing on the positive. The group home was just a transition. Still, the vast unknown future seemed huge to her fragile soul; and she took deep breaths, waiting for the next part of her journey to begin.

AFTER ABOUT THIRTY MINUTES of waiting, Hannah approached a hospital staffer and asked her if the outpatient van was coming.

"You have to register at outpatient first before you can get a ride," said the assistant.

"Where is outpatient?" she asked.

"Outside the front and around the corner of the building next door."

Apparently, by mistake, Hannah assumed she was where she was supposed to be. Grant didn't tell her that she would have to walk to the outpatient lobby. After saying thank you to the staffer, Hannah heaved her full plastic bag over her shoulder and exited the main hospital, feeling wary and totally alone.

She walked about a hundred yards to the outpatient building, beads of sweat trickling down her forehead, her hair noticeably unkempt. She looked like she had just walked out of an insane asylum, which ironically was exactly what she had just done. She hiked up her nice dress slacks awkwardly and periodically as she walked. Her blouse was now noticeably too large for her; and a mop of curly hair, desperate for some anti-frizz gel, completed her look.

Each step farther from the main hospital left her feeling more apprehensive about the security of her situation. She walked purposely, afraid, but hoping for the best. She had endured a difficult journey in the inpatient hospital, and now she was about to enter another.

2

The Group Home

HANNAH TRIED TO BREATHE off the anxiety that was increasing in her body with every moment. She felt very unsure about her present situation. After leaving the main hospital building, Hannah reached the outpatient building and opened the door to outpatient services. She peered in and saw no one there.

"Hello?" she called. No one responded.

Hannah penetrated the hall and knocked on a door that read, "Staff Only." A male nurse opened the door. His name, "Edward," was stitched neatly on his nurse's uniform. He looked orderly and efficient, holding a clipboard and pen in hand. He was a stocky, masculine man and held his shoulders back when he walked. He had a small ponytail pulled neatly to the back of his neck. Hannah noticed that he wore colorful, designer tennis shoes with his nurse's uniform.

"Hi. I'm coming from the main hospital, and I need to take the van to my group home," Hannah said.

"The vans have already left. No one is here now."

"Oh, okay. Um. . . what do you suggest I do?"

"Do you have the number of a family member you can call to come get you?" the nurse asked.

All of Hannah's muscles seized for a moment. She shook her head. She was suddenly without resources. She did not have a phone, and the phone numbers she did have were long distance. Outpatient was closed for the day, and she was totally on her own. Apparently seeing the tension in her face, Edward asked for her full name.

"Hannah Truefield," she said.

"Let me check with the main hospital about your status."

"Thanks."

Edward walked back down the hall. Hannah sat down in the outpatient lobby, dropped her bag to her feet, and tried to stay calm. She was now officially homeless. Hannah felt sure that God would not abandon her now, after everything she had endured in the past month in inpatient treatment. She leaned back in her chair, took a deep breath, tried to think positive thoughts, and waited— something she would have to do more of in the very near future.

Seated in the lobby, Hannah ran possible options through her head of what she should do. She couldn't call a taxi or take the bus because she didn't have any money. Even if she did have the cash, she didn't know where the group home was, exactly. She couldn't call her family because they all lived out of town. Would she end up on the street? Just as her worries began to feed themselves into even bigger worries, the nurse came back to see her.

"Your group homeowner is coming to get you."

"Oh, great. Thanks." She let out a deep sigh, relieved.

Twenty minutes passed. Her knee bounced up and down at a furious pace. She hoped she would make a good impression. She meditated on the Van Gogh print she had just observed in the main lobby of the hospital, concentrating on its peaceful elements. For the next ten minutes, Hannah thought about what Amy, the hospital staffer, said about the oak tree blowing in the wind and about the tree's roots. She was feeling that proverbial wind blowing fiercely right now. She thought about her roots—how she was raised, how she depended on her faith for everything, how she believed that good can come out of bad experiences.

Just then, in walked a shapely, attractive woman with big bottle-red curly hair and a jangling key chain around her neck, holding about ten keys. She was adorned with long, dangly earrings, jeans, and a loud, colorful blouse. Most noticeable was her petite, five-foot-two frame and that hair, that fiery red, curly hair. Her fair skin showed lots of freckles on her arms. Hannah assumed her face probably had freckles under her makeup, too. Hannah stood up, anxious to meet her future advocate for the first time.

The flamboyant woman came straight to her. "How are you?" she asked Hannah, as if they had already met. Her full, sticky red lips gave way to a bright, encouraging smile. "I'm Ms. Rosie."

"Hi," Hannah answered, realizing that this woman was her only link to the outside world. Hannah quickly grabbed hold of her garbage bag suitcase and followed Ms.

Rosie out the front door, saying goodbye to the nurse who helped her.

"Thanks for your help," she told him.

"No problem. See you in outpatient on Monday."

"Okay."

Hannah got in the SUV that would take her to her new, temporary home. Ms. Rosie turned on the radio, which flooded the car with a strong rhythm of classic rock.

Ms. Rosie sang loud to a rock and roll tune. She sang deep and purposefully, punctuating each syllable with passion. She looked over and smiled a broad grin at Hannah. Hannah smiled weakly, rested back in her seat, and took a deep breath. She let out the air slowly. She looked out the window, searching for something positive in her mind to think about.

"Do you have a folder from the nurse?" asked Ms. Rosie.

"No, ma'am," answered Hannah.

"They didn't discharge you with a folder of information?"

"No, ma'am. But I have my discharge paper."

"Let me see it."

Hannah handed her the sweaty, wrinkled paper.

"We need to go pick up your meds."

As they drove through the city, they didn't speak. Hannah listened to the classic rock and thought about her past. She thought about high school and how driven she was then. An above-average student, a good athlete, an extracurricular maniac, Hannah had everything going for her. As a fresh-faced college student, Hannah had worked at a summer camp in the mountains of Tennessee, after her freshman year. She had pushed herself very hard, keeping up with a fast pace, keeping up with young kids. One evening, when she was in the lodge of the camp where they ate dinner, she hit her head on the mantle of a fireplace, and she spent a day resting to recover. During her recuperation from this minor concussion, she struggled to focus or concentrate. At age nineteen, this sign was the first indication of her illness.

After camp was over and she returned to classes for her sophomore year of college, she was very depressed. At the age of twenty, she was seated in a Spanish class in college, trying to do a simple homework assignment. Almost out of the blue, she could not concentrate, which felt very weird to her. She normally focused well when she needed to, but Hannah realized that she couldn't do the simple homework exercises presently before her. She couldn't think. She felt dumb. She felt out of control. Her illness was developing further as indicated by her inability to control her thoughts.

Of course, at the time, Hannah didn't know what was going on with her body, with the neurotransmitters in her brain, and with the lack of focus she seemed to be suffering. In her first inpatient hospital stay, her doctor at the time was not able to discern the source of the problem. Hannah wasn't diagnosed with a specific mental illness until her mid-twenties during her second inpatient hospital stay. By then, her illness was full-blown. Now, in her late twenties, she had just completed her third hospital stay.

She hoped this time she could get a grip on her illness and become as productive and independent as possible.

MS. ROSIE AND HANNAH RODE across town for about thirty minutes. Hannah watched as they passed neighborhoods and streets that she didn't recognize. They were in the large, busy metropolis of Houston, Texas; and good neighborhoods led to shady neighborhoods and back again. The area they drove in was a lower middle class section of town.

The speakers in the car shook with each beat of the song that played on the radio. Eventually, they arrived at a small building which was a pharmacy—a very important contact in Hannah's life. They both got out of the car and walked inside. Hannah felt awkward and unsettled to be in a public place after being sequestered in the inpatient hospital for a month. She fidgeted constantly, sensing that the transition to living on the outside was going to be difficult. She wanted to look in a mirror and fix her hair.

"We only have the first three meds," said the pharmacy tech. "The hospital didn't call in the fourth one. You will have to talk to your doctor's office after the weekend on Monday to get them to call the prescription in."

"Okay. Thank you," said Ms. Rosie.

Hannah swallowed hard. *Monday?* Thoughts raced through her unsettled mind. She would have to wait three whole days to get more of the miracle medicine that was still new in her system. She suddenly felt her sanity being threatened. How would she cope without the main medicine that kept her from hearing voices—the medicine that literally kept her sane? The possibility of going back into a psychosis frightened her. She couldn't possibly go through the horrible experience again of being bombarded by voices she couldn't control. She grew more and more worried as they got back in the car and headed across town.

"Is there any way we can call Dr. Mitchell to try and get the last med I need?" Hannah asked.

"Dr. Mitchell can't be reached right now since it's the weekend," answered Ms. Rosie.

"But I really need this medicine. Can we call the emergency line?"

"She may charge you if she doesn't consider it an emergency. Do you have a credit card?"

"No, ma'am."

"We will just have to wait until Monday."

Hannah wasn't satisfied, fearful of losing her mind again, fearful of having to go back into the main hospital, but she couldn't do anything about her meds now. She breathed deeply, holding each breath for several seconds before a big exhale. Coping skills were really going to have to come through for her if she was going to survive the weekend.

"Okay. So, here are the rules," said Ms. Rosie, interrupting Hannah's worried thoughts. "Curfew during the week is 9:00 p.m.; during the weekend, 11:00 p.m."

"Yes, ma'am."

"And hygiene is very important. When you come home from your program, you take a shower and get cleaned up."

"Yes, ma'am."

"After you come home, you put your dirty clothes in the hamper, you take your shower, and you put on your pajamas."

"Yes, ma'am."

"I'm glad you came here. Your brother is a really nice guy."

Hannah's brother, Michael, had gone ahead of Hannah and provided the down payment for the first month of Hannah's stay at The Refuge, as the group home was called. He was a good brother.

The SUV pulled into an older neighborhood and eventually onto a cracked cement driveway. The car stopped just in front of several men seated in the garage, some of them smoking cigarettes. Hannah lumbered out of the car, grabbed her bag of belongings from the back seat, and walked towards the men. She introduced herself to the ones slumped over in their chairs at the front of the garage.

One guy she noticed was wearing a baseball cap, a tight white T-shirt, Wrangler blue jeans, and brown roper boots. Hannah walked toward him and introduced herself. He said his name was Colt. He had a scruffy goatee, red hair, a handsome face, and startling green eyes. She also met a tall, muscular man named Sydney and a guy sitting next to him named Sam, who was very short in stature and gestured rather awkwardly. Several others that she didn't meet were seated farther back in the garage, puffing out smoke like machines, desperate for the nicotine calm.

Just as Hannah started for the door to the house, Ms. Rosie called to her.

"You are staying in the house across the street with the other women. This is the men's house."

"Oh, okay," said Hannah.

She made a detour and walked across the street. She opened the door of the two-story house, and the smell of fried chicken from the kitchen hit her as she stood in the entryway. A dark, dimly lit den opened just to the right of her. The cable television was at a low volume, and Hannah took a seat in the dark on a heavily pillowed couch. There was no welcome committee.

She looked around the room. The area was stylish. The curtains matched the pillows on the sofa. The wall décor was a collection of nice paintings with similar colors as the curtains. The TV was up to date.

A woman dressed completely in black descended the stairs and walked to the back of the house. Hannah noticed her as she walked by. Another woman came down the stairs. She was wearing sweatpants and a white T-shirt. She cautiously approached Hannah in the den and spoke.

"Are you the new girl?" she asked.

"Uh, I guess so," answered Hannah.

"Hi, I'm Torrie."

"I'm Hannah."

"You coming from the hospital?"

"Yeah."

"I hate the hospital."

"Me too."

Torrie took a seat on the sofa next to Hannah. She stared at the TV. She was a bleached blonde with straight locks of hair and brown eyes. She wore glasses and had a short, athletic build.

"Want to watch some football?" asked Torrie.

"Sure."

"I really like football. Watching those big, bulky guys."

"Yeah. I like it, too," said Hannah.

"Where are you from?" asked Torrie.

"South Louisiana. What about you?"

"Oh, I live just outside of Houston."

The woman in black came back and ascended the stairs, which creaked with every step. Regular traffic throughout the house was obviously the norm for a group home. Torrie warily looked at the woman in black and turned to speak to Hannah in a whisper.

"Watch out for her. That's Amanda. She's as mean as a snake."

Hannah watched a bit fearfully as Amanda ascended the stairs. She was a heavyset woman with short, cropped, black hair.

"Okay, thanks." Hannah was grateful for the warning.

Just then, a somewhat heavyset, forty-something man with a thick, black beard and mustache came in the front door and saw Hannah and Torrie sitting in the dark. He wore a preppy golf shirt hanging over his stomach and his blue jeans. He spoke to Hannah.

"Hi, are you Hannah?"

"Yes, sir."

"I'm Paul, your house manager. Ms. Rosie wants you to get your shower. I'm cooking supper, and your food will be ready soon. Let me show you your bed."

Hannah got up and immediately followed him. She spoke to Torrie as she was leaving the room.

"Nice to meet you, Torrie."

"You, too."

Hannah headed upstairs after Mr. Paul, lugging her bag of belongings with her. The air got warmer and warmer with each upward step. They entered a stuffy, crowded bedroom with two single beds and an air mattress.

"You will be on the air mattress for a couple of weeks. It's only temporary. Your brother brought you a foot-locker. It's in the closet over here," said Mr. Paul.

Hannah nodded and took in the scene. Amanda was lying on her bed in front of a window on the back wall. A thin woman walked in. She appeared to be in her thirties and wore a purple bob wig, heavy purple eye shadow, and long, fake purple nails.

"Oh, come on! She movin' in here, Paul? There ain't enough room here just for the two of us!" she exclaimed.

"No kidding," said Amanda. Amanda spoke with a rough, coarse voice.

Mr. Paul spoke. "Hush up. That's enough. She will sleep on this mattress until Georgie moves out. That's the way it's going to be."

"Aw, shoot. Ain't never going to have any privacy. Not ever. Shoot," said the thin woman.

"Hush up. Dinner will be ready soon. Make sure you wash up. Come see the bathroom, Hannah."

Hannah obediently followed Mr. Paul into the shotgun bathroom.

"Towels here. Hamper right here."

"Thanks," said Hannah.

"I will call everyone when supper is ready."

"Okay."

Hannah came back into the bedroom and sat on the inflated mattress, which crushed inward as she sat on it. She tried not to make eye contact with her new, frustrated roommates. She began to feel very fearful and insecure. She was glad she met Torrie, but these two women obviously did not want her around. Tears welled up in Hannah's eyes, and she fought to keep them from pouring out. She didn't want to cry because the more she cried, the farther away from home she would feel. She closed her eyes and gritted her teeth, wishing she was at home now, more than ever.

3

Getting Acclimated

FIGHTING BACK TEARS, Hannah gathered some courage and spoke with her new roommates at The Refuge.

"I'm sorry to crowd your space, you guys. I'm Hannah."

The woman in purple garb spoke. "I'm Daphney. I really need a cigarette. You got a cigarette?"

"Shut up, Daphney. Can't you tell she's not a smoker?" said Amanda. She then addressed Hannah. "You're probably afraid to smoke, huh?"

"Mind your own business!" yelled Daphney.

Hannah spoke. "I don't smoke because I don't want to."

"See? Told you," spouted Amanda.

"Oh, well. I'm ready for some chicken. You like chicken?" asked Daphney to Hannah.

"Yes, I love it," said Hannah.

"Oh, okay. I was gonna ask if I could have yours if you didn't want it."

"Seriously, Daphney?" said Amanda.

"Shut up," said Daphney.

Hannah spoke again, trying to defuse the tension.

"Actually, I'm pretty hungry after all that hospital food."

"You just coming from the hospital?" asked Daphney.

"Yeah. Twenty-eight days."

"Twenty-eight days?" said Amanda. "What's wrong with you?"

"Leave her alone," said Daphney, firmly. Then she spoke to Hannah. "I been here three years. I'm so tired of being here. I want to move back to Florida. My family's in Florida. You ever been to Florida?"

"She doesn't care, Daphney," said Amanda.

Hannah immediately spoke. She was getting tired of Amanda speaking for her. "What part of Florida are you from?" she asked Daphney.

A call from downstairs interrupted them.

"Ladies! Dinner! Y'all come on!" shouted Mr. Paul.

Daphney and Amanda stood up immediately as if on cue and headed downstairs. Hannah followed them. Amanda, who was just in front of Hannah, turned around and faced Hannah.

"I just got one thing to say to you. Stay out of my business," she said menacingly, breathing bad breath in Hannah's face.

"No problem," said Hannah quickly, trying not to inhale.

As the women moved to go to supper, the beat of their heavy feet shook the squeaky, overused staircase.

They joined the rest of the women in the house at the dining table. Hannah took a seat at the most available option and waited patiently. The food smelled delicious. Hannah was constantly hungry due to the side effects of her medicine, and she welcomed the down-home southern cooking about to greet her taste buds.

They ate in silence. Apparently, eating at The Refuge was serious business. Ms. Rosie walked into the kitchen while they were eating.

"Y'all make sure you clean your plates. I don't want to waste any food. Anybody want seconds?"

Several "yes, ma'ams" were heard; and Ms. Rosie obliged by scooping out more macaroni and cheese. Hannah ate quickly, almost too quickly, and finished while everyone was only halfway through their meal.

"Y'all wait for your medicine. Don't go upstairs until I give them out," ordered Ms. Rosie.

Hannah stared at her empty plate. She didn't want to make eye contact with anyone. In the past, she had never sat down at dinner with so many strangers. She fidgeted in her chair. Torrie was seated next to Hannah, and she spoke to a woman with curly bleached-blonde hair, sitting across the table.

"You're not supposed to bring your hairbrush to the table. That's not clean."

"Mind your own business, Torrie," snapped the woman.

"I'm just saying that you should keep that stuff in your room, Carla," said Torrie.

"Don't tell me what to do!" spouted Carla.

"I'm not telling you…"

"Hey! Hey!" shouted Carla jabbing her finger across the table in Torrie's face, trying to intimidate her with aggression and make Torrie stop talking.

"Don't point your finger at me, creep!" demanded Torrie.

"I'm not a creep!"

Ms. Rosie interrupted the fight. "Okay, okay, settle it down. Y'all stop."

Carla objected. "I don't like it when people tell me what to do!" she snarled.

"Okay, all right. That's enough. Y'all finish your food," said Ms. Rosie.

The two women stopped talking but appeared to be inwardly seething.

Tough crowd, thought Hannah.

Ms. Rosie took her noisy key chain and unlocked the pantry where she kept the medicine. She pulled out eight boxes with names on them. Each box was divided into seven smaller boxes to represent the days of the week, Sunday through Saturday. Ms. Rosie emptied out the appropriate medicine, one by one, and dropped them into the palms of each woman. They each said "thank you," as she gave them out. Hannah then got up and put her plate in the sink.

"Thank you, Mr. Paul. The food was delicious," Hannah said to her efficient house manager, who was diligently working on cleaning the dishes.

"Uh huh. Thank you," said Mr. Paul.

Hannah climbed up the stairs and pulled her footlocker out of the bathroom closet while Amanda and Daphney were still downstairs. She sat on her blow-up mattress and turned the appropriate combination on the lock of the box. At a former hospital visit, her brother had given her the combination to open it. She found a small box inside with a cell phone in it and an envelope holding twenty dollars in cash. Michael had generously left the money for her. She quickly folded the dollars and put them back in the box. Finding the mattress uncomfortable, she put the locked footlocker back in the closet and headed downstairs to rest in the den, her phone in hand.

As she sat in the dimly lit room, she closed her eyes and began to breathe deep breaths and meditate. She read in the prayer book her brother had given her when she was in the main hospital. Hannah spoke prayers in her mind to the God she loved, the God who pulled her out of insanity, and the God who would help her to get through this transition in the group home.

As Hannah meditated, she thought about how her most recent episode had begun. Her illness had grown to a volcanic peak one month earlier. At home, she had worked herself into a manic state, working very hard at her job. Then the voices came, tormenting her; and she became so distraught that she just couldn't handle the struggle anymore on her own.

At that time, Hannah had approached her dad and told him about the voices. He had led her to the kitchen table, where she had sat down next to her mom. Begging them not to take her to the hospital, Hannah had been alert enough to have a conversation. Still, she was stuck in a maddening alternate reality, a psychosis, unable to escape the voices battling with her self-talk. The next morning, Hannah and her mom and dad had piled into the car and headed for Houston to see her doctor.

In her distressed mental state, the four-hour ride was merciless. Hannah had remained focused and intense the entire time they were on the road, trying to be alert to the battle going on in her head. The voices increased in her mind and confused her. When she finally saw her doctor, the physician knew that Hannah absolutely needed inpatient hospital care. Going in for treatment was inevitable. Hannah voluntarily committed herself. During her stay, she didn't know what her next step would be until she finally succumbed to going to the group home, The Refuge.

SHE WATCHED THE news until she felt numb, sometimes closing her eyes and meditating on a peaceful scene in her mind. After about an hour, Hannah trudged upstairs to go to bed. The blow-up mattress was doomed for failure. As soon as she lay down on it, air started to slowly seep out. After a couple of hours, she was lying with one side of the mattress flat on the floor. Mr. Paul was keeping tabs on her, and he faithfully came in to refill the mattress in the middle of the night. This refilling was repeated several times, so Hannah didn't get much sleep. Neither did the other two women in the room.

At six o'clock on an early Saturday morning, Hannah got up and headed downstairs.

"Stupid people. Can't get no sleep around here," said Amanda, hearing Hannah scuffle around.

Daphney looked up from her bed, lifted her pillow and covered her head and ears with it. She sighed dramatically. Mr. Paul had coffee brewing, and Hannah helped herself to a cup of caffeine. Thirty minutes later, Torrie came downstairs to pour herself a cup of coffee, as well. Hannah sat at the table with her. Torrie started suddenly into a discourse, catching Hannah off guard.

"I have to watch my back because I'm in the Witness Protection Program," said Torrie.

Hannah didn't know what to say. "Really?" she finally responded.

"I worked on criminal cases with the FBI. I automatically went into the Witness Protection Program when I worked a case where one of the perps shot me in the head. It caused serious brain damage. That's why I'm here," said Torrie.

"Gosh. I'm sorry."

"Yeah. That's why I can't tell people my real name. My identification is under a different name."

"Do you have any family?" asked Hannah.

"Yeah, but they don't know where I am. I can't tell them where I am for my protection and for theirs."

"My family knows where I am, but they can't take care of me, at least not right now," said Hannah.

"Yeah. That's hard. I wish I was back home. I wish I was back home so bad."

"How long have you been living here?"

"Three months," said Torrie.

"Where do you go during the day, uh, if you don't mind me asking?"

"I go to a center."

"What do you do there?" asked Hannah.

"I color pictures and write all of my information on the backs of them. Then I turn them in to the group therapist," said Torrie.

"That's all you do?"

"We have an hour of group therapy every day."

The two women sat for some time in silence. Hannah eventually went back upstairs to change into her clothes for the day. Then she went downstairs into the den to watch football. Her brother was coming today to visit her from out of town. While waiting for him, she passed the time by reading her prayer book and meditating on what she read. Around eight o'clock that morning, just as she was hoping he would come, she heard a knock on the front door. Hannah got up quickly to answer it.

"Hey, sis."

"Hey, Michael."

"How's it going?"

"I'm hanging in there," said Hannah.

"Let's see if we can't get your meds today, okay?"

"Okay."

So far, she had only spent one night at The Refuge and maintained her precarious sanity by meditating, reading, and watching the news. Since today was Saturday, Hannah was grateful for her brother's visit. Michael was an incredibly responsible, caring person. If anyone could get her medicine straightened out, Michael could.

Michael's wife, Jessica, came too and was waiting for them in the car. Jessica was a pretty, fifty-something woman with a bright, big smile and short, soft brown hair. The three occupied a small, green sedan and took off to brave the cement jungle of intersecting highways stretching out across the city, population over two million. Hannah's athletically built brother with a full head of auburn hair and a full auburn beard manned the car with great intent and purpose.

Michael was immediately on the phone, trying to talk to a pharmacist. They were on their way to get some Tex-Mex cuisine from a nearby restaurant. At the restaurant, Hannah realized her personal struggle in ordering food and tried to keep her thoughts together. Jessica helped to pass the time by showing Hannah how to use her new phone that Michael had given her. She recommended that Hannah charge her phone every night to make sure it was ready for use each day. The phone was not a smart phone; it was a flip phone, so Hannah couldn't listen to music on it. Michael had also given Hannah an MP3 player with some relaxing, spiritual music that she could concentrate on when she needed it.

After lunch, the brave trio headed to the store to pick up some things that Hannah needed. At the store, Hannah fidgeted nervously, feeling weird again to be out and about in such a large public place. When they entered the heavily populated store, she was in for a challenge to try to focus and concentrate with so many people around. She didn't do well in crowds. She felt afraid. Michael and Jessica cut her loose to let her explore some and shop while they went to look for some things for her. She got shampoo, lotion, toothpaste, a toothbrush, shower gel, facial hair remover cream, and other essentials. Michael kept his eye on her occasionally and helped her to be more conservative with the size of toiletries that she selected.

After about forty-five minutes, they arrived at the checkout counter. Hannah was feeling very uneasy, and she wrung her hands back and forth nervously. She became so uncomfortable that Jessica finally walked her out to the car where they waited until Michael finished checking out. Jessica entertained Hannah by showing her pictures on her phone.

After much driving around town, Michael came up short for the medicine that Hannah needed that weekend. They were all disappointed. Hannah was struggling to concentrate and really wished she had that precious medicine in her system, but they had hit a bureaucratic wall of rules and regulations that prevented her from getting the medicine she needed from the pharmacy. To expect to get any medicine on a weekend when the doctor's office was closed was just impossible. Her goal of staying sane was threatened. Michael and Jessica took her back to the house with her new things, for which she was very grateful.

When they were saying goodbye, Hannah couldn't hold back the tears. Michael tried to comfort her.

"I'm sorry I couldn't get your meds. I'm really sorry I couldn't get them," said Michael, his eyes tearing up as well.

"That's okay. You did a lot for me today." She looked deeply into Michael's eyes to make sure he believed it. Her face streaming with tears, his eyes welling up, they shared a very special moment as brother and sister. She loved him so much. He loved her deeply, too.

Grateful for both her brother and sister-in-law, Hannah gave them hugs, and they left. She had two more nights of the weekend before she could get her critical medicine. Clinging to her sanity deliberately and carefully, she focused on her prayer book and read the scriptures slowly.

She greatly feared that the voices would return to attack her mind. Why did she listen to them? The answer was simple: the voices were so intrusive and interruptive that they prevented her from functioning normally. When she was in a psychosis, she became so preoccupied with the voices in her head that she isolated herself from everyone. She just couldn't handle being in her head and in the world at the same time. Balancing two different realities—one inside her mind and the other outside her mind—she felt oppressed and distraught because the voices kept talking to her constantly. She felt as if she was a prisoner of war caught behind enemy lines and was being tortured in her mind. When going through a psychotic episode of her illness, her only relief was sleeping sedated at night with medicine in her system.

Seated in the den at the group home, Hannah clung to the music from her MP3 player that was pouring into her mind the way a baby clutches onto a blanket, trusting and open. She was grateful that her mind was free, but she feared potential insanity encroaching upon her once more. She struggled to hang on for just a little while longer.

4

Amanda

AMANDA WORE A SERIOUS, intense frown on her face. Her arms were folded in a posture of defiance. Saturday night was upon The Refuge, and Ms. Rosie was in the process of twisting Amanda's arm to give up her bed for a few nights to let Hannah sleep there. Hannah was sitting in her spot on the couch in the den. She could hear Amanda and Ms. Rosie talking at the dining table in the next room. Hannah was trying to read her prayer book.

"So, how are you doing, Amanda?" asked Ms. Rosie.

"I'm okay," she said reluctantly.

"Are you making any friends at the new center you've been going to?"

"Aw, Ms. Rosie, you know I keep to myself."

"It's good to have a few friends."

"I don't need them."

"I qualify as a friend, don't I?"

"Sure, Ms. Rosie, but you're different."

"How so?"

"You look out for me."

"You've been here what—four years now?" asked Ms. Rosie.

"Four years this February," said Amanda.

"Do you remember how you felt when you first got here?"

"Well, it's been a while, Ms. Rosie."

"Ah, I bet you can remember. I remember you being this scared little kitten who needed a home."

"That was a long time ago," said Amanda.

"I remember how long it took you to trust me."

"Yes, ma'am."

"Remember when we were so crowded in the house, and one of the girls gave up her bed for a few nights so you could sleep in a real bed instead of on the sofa?"

"Yes. I remember. She was a nice person."

"Well, I'm asking you to do the same for Hannah."

"Oh, Ms. Rosie."

"Now, Amanda, it's only for a few days."

"But Ms. Rosie, I don't like her. She's too quiet. Too suspicious."

"Well, maybe she's just scared like you were when you first got here. Did you ever think about that?"

"You're not really asking me to be friends with her, right?"

"Only if you want to."

"I don't trust the quiet ones. They are usually up to something."

"Maybe she's just learning her environment. Give her a chance, Amanda," Ms. Rosie implored.

Amanda was quiet for a moment, then she spoke. "And I just have to give up my bed for a few nights?"

"That's right."

"Well, I won't do it for her, but I will do it for you."

"Fair enough."

"Can you please tell her? I don't want to talk to her."

"Okay, Amanda."

So, albeit reluctantly, Amanda agreed. After talking with Ms. Rosie, she went back upstairs to get some things she needed before she went to sleep downstairs on the couch. Ms. Rosie then walked into the den where Hannah was sitting. Hannah looked up and saw her approach. Ms. Rosie sat on the couch next to Hannah.

"Hey, Hannah."

"Hi, Ms. Rosie."

"I need to talk to you."

"Okay."

"I need to talk to you about Amanda. Now, Amanda is rough around the edges, I know. But she has her reasons."

"Okay." Hannah was waiting for an explanation.

"She doesn't have a very good track record of making friends here," said Ms. Rosie.

"How come?"

"She would just start to make a friend, and then they would end up leaving The Refuge and move on."

"And Amanda was left here with no one."

"Right."

"I guess I can understand. But does she have to be so tough?" asked Hannah.

"Sometimes being in a group home for a long time while others come and go can be hard on a person. Amanda has been here about four years. She has nowhere else to go. Can you understand why that might make her kind of tough?"

"Yes, ma'am. I mean, I guess so."

"Well, even in her toughness, Amanda has agreed to let you sleep in her bed for a few nights so you won't have to wrestle with the air mattress, okay?"

"She would do that for me? Are you sure?" asked Hannah.

"Well, actually, she's doing it out of respect for me."

"She doesn't like me, does she?"

"Well, I just think she doesn't know you yet, so she doesn't trust you. Just give it some time and respect the veteran that she is here."

"Okay, Ms. Rosie. Thank you."

"Sure. Sleep well."

Even though she knew that Amanda hadn't given up her bed for Hannah personally, Hannah felt the gesture was incredibly generous. In a group home, the only thing that a person can really claim as their own space is their bed. By giving up her bed, Amanda was moving completely out of her comfort zone.

After speaking with Hannah in the den, Ms. Rosie left to go into the dining room to organize paperwork. Hannah looked up to see Amanda walk into the den. She began to make a bed for herself on one of the couches.

Hannah spoke gingerly, "Thanks for letting me sleep in your bed. Are you going to be okay down here?"

"You don't need to know that!" Amanda snapped.

Hannah didn't utter another word, guessing that Amanda was letting her know to stay out of her business again. Hannah silently retreated to her loaner bed upstairs, scared but grateful. She got settled in for the night. As she lay down, she plugged her ears with earbuds from her MP3 player. She needed to listen to some soothing music to drown out the television that blared from the corner of the room. Daphney, who was lying in the bed next to her, was listening to the television that was turned on loud to late-night comedy hour. Hannah listened to a modern hymn and felt the music wash over her, calming her unsettled spirit.

"The Lord is my shepherd. I won't be wanting. I won't be wanting," played the song.

Hannah felt at ease with the gentle, poetic melody; and she immediately closed her eyes. She took deep breaths and pictured a sweeping pasture with beautiful, colorful trees at the peak of fall. She imagined herself sitting on a wooden bench, breathing in deeply the fragrant autumn air.

Eventually, Daphney turned off the program on TV and went to sleep. Hannah took out her earbuds and nodded off herself. She embraced the stillness, her body enveloped with the effects of sedation from prescription drugs, although she was still missing that one very effective one.

SUNDAY MORNING ARRIVED quickly. Hannah woke up early, startled to feel a shadow standing over her.

She looked up and saw Carla hovering over her. Hannah jumped out of bed quickly.

"What are you doing?" demanded Hannah, her voice shaking, her mind still half asleep.

Carla didn't answer, but she just stood there with a creepy smile on her face.

"Get away from me," said Hannah firmly, feeling the back of her neck getting hot.

Carla didn't move, still smiling.

"I said get away from me!" yelled Hannah, now raising her voice deliberately.

Carla slunk away smiling, just as they heard Mr. Paul's voice from downstairs.

"Get up, ladies! Come get your medication!"

Shaken, Hannah followed the other women downstairs, determined to let Mr. Paul know about Carla. After Carla went outside for a smoke, Hannah spoke to him.

"Mr. Paul, I have to tell you something."

"Okay."

"Carla was standing over me when I woke up. It gave me the creeps, like she was about to do something to me."

"Oh, okay. I'll keep an eye out for her. I'm glad you told me."

After she took care of Carla, Hannah began to worry about the meds she was taking. She sensed that something was wrong. The number of pills that she just swallowed that morning wasn't the same as what was given to her in the main hospital. She pointed that out to Mr. Paul, and he told her to talk to Ms. Rosie across the street about her meds.

Hannah walked to the men's house, looking for her group homeowner. She found the energetic woman cleaning one of the bathrooms.

"Whatcha need?" asked Ms. Rosie, mopping the floor vigorously, distracted by her work.

"Ms. Rosie, I don't think my meds are right."

"Why? I filled the box according to your prescriptions."

"Well, there are a couple of pink pills that I didn't take when I was in the main hospital. Can I check the meds in my basket?"

"I'll let you look at them tonight before you take them again."

"Okay. Thank you."

Hannah walked back to her house, wringing her hands. She was worried and anxious because she didn't have the main medicine that initially pulled her out of her insanity while she was in the inpatient hospital. She knew she needed to be her own biggest advocate, since her parents and brother were not there the whole time to fight for her. She had to learn to fight for herself. She said a quick prayer that she would get her last important medicine on Monday. Her hopes to maintain her sanity were strong.

Hannah parked herself in the den of The Refuge, taking up the space as if it were her own, since she really didn't officially have her own space yet. The couch on which Amanda slept the previous night was straightened up with all the pillows in place. Amanda was nowhere to be found. Hannah kept a duffel bag with her. Her brother, Michael, had given it to her to keep some things close to her. She carried the bag with her everywhere, afraid that it might get stolen if she left it somewhere in the house. The bag held all her important paperwork—copies of her driver's license and her insurance cards. Earlier, her mom had faxed the paperwork to Michael, who had given it to Hannah the day before, during their outing to the store. Jessica, her sister-in-law, had found Hannah a small purse when they were out shopping, which Hannah always kept with her as well, hiding her phone inside of it.

While Hannah sat in the den, she watched a football game. Watching football made her feel somewhat safe because she used to watch the sport with her dad, and the game reminded her of him. Hannah adored her father. He was a generous, kind, gentle soul; and he was there for her the last two times she was in a psychiatric hospital. In the past, when she was hospitalized, her dad visited her every day, walking with her around the hospital campus. Now, her dad was quite fragile, walking with a walker and seeming a bit confused occasionally, showing his symptoms of Parkinson's. He couldn't be there for her now like he had been in the past. She felt very lonely without him.

As she watched the football game, she imagined her father sitting in his khaki trousers, white Hanes T-shirt, and flip-flops, giving commentary as the game progressed.

"They say that quarterback almost won the Heisman trophy," he would say.

Hannah kept thinking about her dad and wished she could fix her illness so she could see him again. Controlling her illness wasn't necessarily all in Hannah's power. She was vulnerable to the kind of meds she was taking, and she depended greatly on her doctor to give her the right balance of medication.

Thankfully, her doctor happened to be brilliant in choosing the right kind of meds for her to take, and Hannah trusted Dr. Mitchell implicitly. She told herself to be patient about the meds, and she focused on the football game, closing her eyes periodically to meditate on a peaceful nature scene.

For most of the day, Hannah concentrated on meditating, practicing breathing exercises, and TV surfing—a few coping skills that helped her along her continual journey to embrace sanity as she knew it. Meditating on Bible verses from her prayer book was particularly helpful to her, as well. She was on her way to surviving the weekend. The day was restful up until the argument that struck the house right about dinner time. As she was flipping the channels in the den, loud yelling erupted from upstairs.

"Shut up, Daphney! I said shut up!" cried Amanda.

"I ain't done nothing to you," said Daphney.

"You're a horrible person, Daphney. You don't care about nobody but yourself!"

The two yelled at each other for some time in the upstairs bedroom, with their voices carrying throughout the house. Hannah felt her stomach drop at the onset of the argument.

"I told you to save me some cigarettes, but you just had to smoke them, didn't you!" yelled Amanda.

"I never said you could have them," said Daphney.

"Well, isn't that hypocritical of you. You promised them to me if I gave you some of my coffee. You make me sick!"

"I ain't never drank none of your coffee!"

Just as the argument escalated, Mr. Paul came in the house, heard the ruckus, and bounded up the stairs.

"That's enough, ladies!" said Mr. Paul. "Y'all come downstairs!"

"She owes me some cigarettes," said Amanda adamantly.

"Y'all got to quit sharing your stuff. You all know that," said Mr. Paul.

"I don't owe her nothing," said Daphney firmly.

"Yes, you do. You're a liar. A stinking, dirty liar!" attacked Amanda.

Mr. Paul interrupted again.

"Let's go downstairs. Now. Come on, let's go."

Daphney and Amanda stomped downstairs. They sat at the kitchen table far from each other with Mr. Paul seated between them. He was presently on the phone with Ms. Rosie. They were seated in the room just opposite the den where Hannah sat. In the dim light, Hannah could see them and hear them talking. Mr. Paul hung up and spoke to the women.

"Ms. Rosie said if you keep sharing your cigarettes, then you will lose your smoking privileges."

Amanda objected. "But she. . ."

"Don't matter what happened up till now," said Mr. Paul. "Let's worry about the present. No more sharing. Ms.

Rosie is serious about this. And y'all got to learn to get along."

The women sat stone-faced. Daphney chewed on her long, fake fingernails, making a clickety-clack sound. Amanda folded her arms tightly to her chest and swung her foot back and forth defiantly under the table.

"Okay, ladies? I got to know you understand."

"Okay," said Daphney reluctantly.

"Okay," said Amanda, her mouth pursed within a tight face.

"You two leave each other alone and move along now. Go find something to do."

The two women immediately stood up and went in opposite directions. Daphney headed across the street to the men's house, heaving a deep sigh on her way out. Amanda went to the back door to cool off outside, slamming the door behind her.

Observing that argument led Hannah to a personal resolution: she was not going to get involved in any kind of drama in the house. Her goal was to be the most cooperative, rule-abiding tenant who minded her own business. Whatever drama there was, she would make sure she was not involved. That purpose did not keep her from watching all the drama at The Refuge, but her resolve did help her to be strong, stay sane, and get better for the future.

HANNAH WAS INCREDIBLY hungry. The side effects of her meds made her crave food more than usual. She moved into the kitchen to talk to Mr. Paul.

"What's for supper, Mr. Paul?"

"Fried fish and french fries."

"Sounds good. Did you catch the fish?"

"Heh. No. Bought it at the store."

"If I didn't know that, I wouldn't have known the difference."

"Heh. True. That's true."

Hannah liked Mr. Paul. He was a sensitive, kind, orderly man. He was a good cook, too. The fish turned out great. Flaky white meat was surrounded by fresh, crispy batter. Portions were large, and Hannah's stomach was satisfied.

Hannah remembered about her medication. After dinner, she asked Mr. Paul if she could look at them. Mr. Paul took his keys and unlocked the closet where all the main medicines were kept. Hannah looked at her meds and the prescription written on each one. She realized that she needed to take some at night instead of in the morning, and she made the correction to her medicine box. Handling her meds in this way made her feel very independent. She took her meds with a glass of water and gave the box back to Mr. Paul.

The next day was Monday, and Hannah was going to her first day in the outpatient program at the hospital. She was glad she was going to have something to do, and she went to sleep with anticipation about what the next day would hold. She longed for that special medicine to get in her system as soon as possible to avoid any chance of a relapse.

5

Outpatient

THE YELL WAS HEARD throughout the house at six a.m. on Monday morning.

"Y'all get up! Time to take your meds!"

For a moment, Hannah didn't know where she was. She opened her eyes and looked around the room. She was in Amanda's bed again, but that fact didn't register in her mind. Feeling disoriented, she saw her roommate, Daphney, get up; and Hannah slowly followed her downstairs.

"Y'all want a snack? Come get your snack," said Mr. Paul.

Powdered doughnuts started her day, and Hannah swallowed them down quickly, feeling the thick, sticky sugar coat the top of her mouth. Hannah also grabbed a cup of coffee brewing in the kitchen. She downed it quickly and headed upstairs to change out of her pajamas. After getting dressed for the day and brushing her teeth, she waited in the den downstairs for her ride to come.

At 7:30 a.m., a horn honked outside.

"Hannah, your ride's here!" called Mr. Paul.

Hannah walked outside towards a long, gray van. She headed for the back of the vehicle, following Colt, Sydney, and Sam from the men's home. The driver stopped her as she was getting in.

"Who are you? I didn't know I was coming to pick you up."

"My name is Hannah. I have my discharge paper."

"Let me see it."

Hannah dug in her duffel bag and pulled out the sheet of paper with her name and medicines listed. The driver inspected the information.

"Okay. You can come on. Usually I know ahead of time who I am picking up. No one told me you were riding with me. Come on. Get in."

"Thank you."

Hannah pursued the back of the van, and she climbed into a space almost too small for her to fit in. She gave herself some space between her and the unshaven man sitting next to her, who was sleeping with his head against the window, headphones over his ears.

They pulled out of the neighborhood and immediately hit the freeway. The ten-passenger van lumbered down the highway, jostling and jumping with every bump in the road. Hannah hoped she would not get nauseous on the ride over there. Packed in among the rest like diced peaches in a fruit cup, Hannah breathed the stuffy, stale air and tried to hold her arms close to her to avoid touching anyone. She liked her space.

After twenty minutes, they arrived at outpatient services; and they squeezed out of the van the way they squeezed in, slowly and one at a time. Hannah breathed relief into the fresh, open air and waited in line to go inside to the outpatient program.

All the patients waited in the lobby of the outpatient clinic. Hannah filled out the appropriate, lengthy paperwork to be admitted for treatment. As she waited, she tried very hard not to make eye contact with anyone, keeping her eyes focused on the floor or on the wall above the heads of the other clients. At 8:30 a.m., she followed the group like cattle, to a room lined with vinyl couches and chairs.

A therapist, Ms. Jordan, was seated in the room and instructed Hannah to fill out a twenty-four-hour check-in sheet. Ms. Jordan was an average-sized, pretty, sensitive person with long, blonde hair. A tenderhearted yet strong woman, she appeared to be in her late twenties.

Hannah was very tired, feeling like her head was underwater. The meds she took at night made her feel that way in the morning, which she grew used to. The new meds that she received in the main hospital made her feel as if the floor was moving beneath her, as if she was on a cruise ship, walking on unsteady ground. As she filled out the twenty-four-hour sheet, she put down how many hours she slept the night before, that she was still hearing voices, and that she was neither suicidal nor homicidal. She also listed what coping skills she was using—listening to music, watching TV, praying, reading, and meditating. This ritual of checking in every day was meant to help her in the future when she eventually checked out of the outpatient program.

Ms. Jordan began to go around the room, asking people to rate themselves on the happiness scale from one to ten. Colt, Sydney, and Sam were all in her group. All three of them said they were a ten on the happiness scale. Hannah looked at the face of each man as they spoke. None of them looked happy to her. Instead, they looked burdened, tired, and worn out from living.

Hannah said she was about a three.

"Why so low, Hannah?" asked Ms. Jordan.

"I don't have all my medicine," answered Hannah.

"Talk to your doctor about it if you see her today."

"Okay."

Since Hannah was in outpatient, she was supposed to see Dr. Mitchell twice a week to keep tabs on how she was doing.

Along with the three men, two other women whom Hannah did not know sat in the group. Their names were Martha and Andrea. Martha was a brunette sixty-something woman with tardive dyskinesia, a condition of side effects where the patient may have a variety of behaviors. In Martha's case, she smacked her lips constantly and subconsciously. Martha said she was a four on the happiness scale. Andrea, a blonde thirty-something woman with a designer warm-up suit to match her tennis shoes, was slouched in her seat, sleeping on the couch.

She must be really doped up with meds, Hannah thought.

Ms. Jordan spoke. "Andrea, I need you to wake up. We are going to talk about our goals right now." Andrea opened her eyes sleepily but did not sit up.

Ms. Jordan continued. "I want everyone to tell me what your goal is for today," she said. "We'll start with you, Sam."

"I want to be positive."

"Okay, good." Ms. Jordan wrote down Sam's goal on the board. "Sydney?"

"I want to smoke just one cigarette today."

"Okay, thank you. Colt?"

"To be a good friend."

"Good. Good goal. Martha?"

"To stay in group."

"Good. Very good. Andrea?"

"To stay awake today."

"That's a good goal. And, Hannah?"

"To live in the present."

"Good. Good goals. These goals are very good. You should be very proud of yourselves. All of you are on the right track."

Ms. Jordan sectioned off half of the erase board for the goals and wrote "Discipline" in the other open blank area on the board.

"Today, our topic is discipline. Can anyone define discipline for me?"

The room was quiet. No one could formulate an answer. After snapping out their goals, the introduction of a new topic like this one made everyone stare at Ms. Jordan in a foggy stupor. Their psychiatric medication seemed to be leaving them in a sudden daze that appeared to rest heavily like a thick cloud in the room.

"Everyone just say what comes to your mind when you hear the word 'discipline,' okay?" The stupor evaporated, and popcorn answers started flowing.

Hannah spoke first. "Order."

"Okay. Good," Ms. Jordan said, writing it on the board. "Anybody else?"

"Structure, like you structure your day," said Colt.

"Right. Good." She wrote "structure" on the board.

Sydney spoke, "It makes me think of the military. I was a Navy SEAL, and we had lots of discipline."

"Okay," said Ms. Jordan. She wrote down "military."

"I was a cop, too. Lots of discipline in the police force, yes, sir," said Sydney.

"Okay." She wrote down "law enforcement." "Thank you. Anyone else? Sam, what do you think when you hear the word 'discipline'?"

"Obeying your parents," said Sam.

"Yes, we can learn discipline from Mom and Dad," said Ms. Jordan. "Anyone else? Andrea, do you have any thoughts?"

A long pause silenced the room. Andrea rocked back and forth in her chair, thinking. "Habits. Habits are formed through discipline."

"Okay. That's true. Discipline defines our habits. What about you, Martha?"

Martha thought a minute while smacking her lips. She finally spoke, "You have to have discipline to teach your kids discipline."

"Good. Training your kids takes discipline. How can we make discipline a part of our everyday life? What can we do to make us have a disciplined life?"

More silence filled the room.

Sydney spoke. "Ms. Jordan. Is it time for breakfast?"

"Oh, right. Thanks for being my timekeeper. Let me check and see if the food is here."

As Ms. Jordan exited the room, Sydney began to talk.

"Yeah, man, those SEALs don't put up with nothing. You've got to suck it up, dig deep, and do those push-ups. No mercy. Absolutely no mercy."

The rest of the room remained quiet. Andrea started to snore, apparently letting herself get lost in sleep. She was already not keeping her goal.

Colt spoke to Hannah. "You get settled in okay at The Refuge with Ms. Rosie?"

"Oh, yeah. Thanks."

"Ms. Rosie's got a big heart. Just remember to respect her, and you will be okay."

"Yeah, okay, thanks. I like her."

"She's cool. And she can cook real good, too. You'll be fine," assured Colt.

Ms. Jordan entered the room. "Y'all come to breakfast."

The six patients stood up, formed a natural line, and exited the room. As they passed each door in the hallway, the drone of discussion could be heard coming from the other individual rooms—an extensive amount of psychotherapy was going on. They walked down the hall to the snack room, and each person got two mini boxes of Fruit Loops and a small carton of milk.

Hannah took a seat next to Colt while she ate breakfast. "So, where are you from?" asked Hannah.

"Born and raised in east Texas," said Colt. "Love hunting in those woods."

"What do you like to hunt?"

"Anything. Squirrels, coons, doves."

"Do you like to fish, too?"

"Oh, yeah."

"What do you fish for?"

"I like catching those striped bass. Sweet."

"Do you like those spinner-bait lures?"

"Oh, yeah. Catch a lot on those."

"What about those black plastic worms? Do they work?"

"Sometimes, if you're lucky." He paused. "How do you know so much about fishing?"

"I used to go fishing with my dad, especially when I was younger," said Hannah.

Hannah liked Colt. He was a man's man, a self-professed redneck, and walked with a noticeable, appealing swagger. Then, of course, there was his tight jaw and his eyes—his green, hypnotic eyes.

After breakfast, everyone scattered. Some went outside to smoke or breathe fresh air. Some went back to the group room to relax. After breakfast, they had fifteen minutes to pass the time before group resumed. Hannah got on the phone with her pharmacy.

A pharmacist answered the phone, and Hannah began to speak.

"Uh, yes. My name is Hannah Truefield, and I'm calling to see if I have any medicine waiting to be picked up."

"Yes, ma'am. They called it in."

"Great. Thanks."

Whatever snafu about her medicine that happened when the main hospital discharged her was obviously corrected. Just then, a counselor from one of the other groups opened a door near where Hannah was standing.

The counselor complained to Hannah. "Can you go away from the rooms when you talk on the phone? I don't think you realize how loud your voice is in the hallway…"

Irritated by the counselor, Hannah walked down the hall abruptly before the counselor could finish her sentence.

Sydney walked up to her. "You got a cigarette?"

"Uh, no. I don't smoke," replied Hannah. Sydney nodded and kept walking.

Hannah walked into the kitchen, got some coffee, and drank it down quickly. Then she sat down in the group room and began to draw on her Styrofoam coffee cup. To kill some time, she drew flowers and leaves in a pretty composition. Then she put the cup on the shelf in the room to display it. Other clients had already put up their colored pictures on the walls for people to see.

"Okay. Let's get back together for group," said Ms. Jordan, reentering the room.

The other patients trickled back into the room.

"We were talking about discipline; and before breakfast, I asked you how you can make discipline a part of your everyday life. Anybody want to take a stab at that?" asked Ms. Jordan. No one answered. After a few moments passed, she summed up the day, giving a speech on discipline that made sense.

"Basically, discipline is doing stuff you don't really want to do, on a regular basis. Some of you got off track with discipline; and now you're here trying to find your way back to a normal life, right? It's somewhat simple. You've got to get up in the morning, dress presentably, stay productive during the day, pay your bills, brush your teeth at night, take a shower, take your meds, and go to bed at a decent hour. You've got to keep a schedule. Committing yourself to discipline will keep you guys out of here—out of the hospital. It all comes down to loving yourself. Love yourself enough to be disciplined, and you have won part of the battle of maintaining a stable life."

On the way back to The Refuge that day, while they were bouncing along in the outpatient van, Hannah thought about what Ms. Jordan said. That's what Hannah needed—a disciplined life. She needed to take care of herself even when she didn't feel like it. These thoughts about discipline gave Hannah hope—hope for a more independent life.

WHEN HANNAH ARRIVED at The Refuge for the afternoon, Ms. Rosie told her that the pharmacy had delivered her medicine to the house. Hannah felt so relieved at this news. That night, with all of her meds securely dissolving in her stomach, Hannah's thoughts were full and deep about her temporary home.

As she lay in her bed, she thought about her day. She also thought about Colt. He seemed to be a nice guy. She wanted to get to know him better but didn't want to rush things. She liked that he was an outdoors, country boy. He seemed to be a strong guy emotionally, even though he was probably going through a hard time, just like Hannah.

Hannah was grateful for the people she met in her outpatient group, even though she didn't know them very well. Even with the newness of relationships among them, they seemed to have a kind of bond. All of them were in an uncomfortable situation. All of them were there to recover from a major life crisis that had disrupted their lives. She was grateful that she could go through this journey with them. She wasn't afraid of them the way she feared the patients in the inpatient hospital.

As she evaluated her thoughts, Hannah realized that the strongest feeling she experienced that night was gratitude. She felt grateful—very, very grateful. The thing that she was most grateful for was a supportive family. She talked to her mom on the phone every day. She talked with her brother on the phone about every other day. She wondered about the clients in her outpatient group. She wondered if they had families to lean on, too. She didn't know what she would do without that kind of support. Having people genuinely care about her recovery made all the difference in motivating herself to keep moving forward, one step at a time. She had many things to be grateful for. Before she drifted off to sleep, she prayed to God about all of them.

"Dear Father in Heaven, thank you for loving me. Thank you for a family who loves me. Thank you that I have a roof over my head. Thank you that I have good food to eat. Thank you that I have a good doctor. Thank you that I have a good group homeowner. Thank you that I got the medicine I needed today. Thank you for everyone in my outpatient group—Colt, Sydney, Sam, Martha, and Andrea. Thank you for the people in my group home too, even though some of them bug me. Help us all to recover well. In Jesus' name, amen."

6

Dr. Mitchell

TUESDAY WAS DOCTOR DAY. The first time that Hannah had met Dr. Mitchell, Hannah was in her mid-twenties. At the time, she was going through an episode of her illness. She was hearing many voices and was losing her mind but didn't know what was wrong or why she was having such serious symptoms. Hannah struggled off and on with her illness for six years before being officially diagnosed. When Hannah was hospitalized at age twenty-five, she surrendered to the care of Dr. Mitchell, who diagnosed Hannah with schizoaffective disorder, a disorder with bipolar symptoms and features of schizophrenia, which are usually hallucinations and delusions in a psychosis. Now, several years later, she had gone back into the hospital for inpatient treatment due to symptoms of her illness; and Dr. Mitchell had rescued her from the clutches of insanity once again.

AT THE GROUP HOME, Hannah got ready that morning the same way she had the day before and eventually arrived on schedule in her meeting room at outpatient therapy. While seated in group, after check-in time and breakfast, the outpatient nurse, Edward, came to the door of Ms. Jordan's meeting room.

Edward spoke firmly. "Hannah, Dr. Mitchell is here to see you."

Hannah nodded and got up quickly, swung her duffel bag and purse over her shoulder, and purposefully followed Edward down the hall. He led her to some chairs lined against the wall in front of the door of a small office. Dr. Mitchell was a serious, business-minded doctor with an enormous amount of compassion. She had a balance of purposeful, direct, sensitive communication compounded with well-chosen administration of medicine. She was a valuable physician.

As she was sitting there waiting to see her, Hannah realized that she respected Dr. Mitchell so much that she treasured her doctor-patient relationship with her. While Hannah was thinking about her past mental health history, a patient walked out of Dr. Mitchell's office. Hannah was up next. She walked into the room, and Dr. Mitchell immediately spoke.

"Hello. How are you?" she asked Hannah.

She was dressed in gray slacks and a blue sweater, understated but classic.

"I'm okay. I could be better," responded Hannah.

"Okay. What's going on?"

"I'm just trying to get into a routine at the group home."

"How's that going?"

"It's okay. I just would rather be home."

"Yes, I can understand that. How's your thinking?"

"I'm thinking much better than when I was in the main hospital last month."

"No suicidal or homicidal thoughts?"

"No, ma'am."

"How's your medicine working?"

"It's okay. Except I didn't get my main medicine until yesterday. I didn't have it the whole weekend."

"Yes, I got your brother's message. The nurse who picked up the shift after your discharge failed to call it in properly."

"I was really worried that I didn't have it."

"I can imagine."

"I'm just thankful that nothing bad happened while I waited for it."

"Me too. How's your appetite?"

"Good, but I can literally feel myself gaining weight. I gained seven pounds last week. The food at the group home is delicious, but I think the large portions combined with the side effects of my medicine are making me fat."

"Okay. Try to exercise if you can."

"Okay." Hannah hated to exercise. Going up and down the stairs at the group home was the extent of her contribution to cardiovascular activity.

"How's your memory?"

"Not so good."

"Moods?"

"I feel kinda down."

"Give the medicine a little more time."

"Okay. How do you feel about me going home eventually?"

"I think you are completely capable of making that decision."

"But do you think it's a good idea to move home?"

Dr. Mitchell paused. "If you move to your hometown, I think it would probably be best to live in an apartment."

"Okay."

"Living on your own will help you to develop your own identity as an independent adult."

"So, you think I could actually live on my own?"

"Absolutely. This program will help get you there. Make sure you pay attention to everything they are teaching you here."

"Yes, ma'am. I want to get better. And I want to do the right thing."

"I know. You've come a long way in one month. Let yourself grow into your new life again. This is not the end. This is just the beginning."

"I just feel so behind in everything, so behind in life."

"Try and be patient with yourself."

"Okay. I keep thinking that my time will run out before I get a chance to reach my destination, before I get a chance to grow up."

"Just take one day at a time. That's all we have strength for, just for today."

"How long does it take to get better?"

"Give yourself a year. Lots of different kinds of recoveries take about a year."

A pause filled the room.

"Do you have any other questions?" asked Dr. Mitchell.

Hannah swallowed hard. She gathered her courage.

"Can you explain to me why my brain works the way it does?"

"What do you mean?"

"Can you tell me why I hear voices during an episode? I only hear them at certain times when I'm really stressed."

Dr. Mitchell paused and hesitated for a moment. She looked seriously at Hannah.

"Okay. Anybody can slip into a psychosis under certain circumstances. When there is too much pressure on our brain or too much stress, the brain can implode; and then these thoughts fire off on their own when you start hearing voices. Then you can't control what you are thinking."

"I feel bad when I can't control my thoughts. I feel like a very bad person."

"You're not bad. You're not bad at all. I think you are a very good person. You judge yourself way too hard."

Hannah's shoulders dropped in a moment of dejection.

"Don't be so hard on yourself," said Dr. Mitchell. Things are going to get better."

"Thanks."

"You're welcome. Do you have any other questions?"

Hannah thought for a moment.

"Hannah?"

Hannah snapped to attention after drifting off in her thoughts. "Yes, ma'am?"

"Do you have any other questions?"

"I have one more question, Dr. Mitchell."

"Okay."

"Is it true that people with bipolar disorder function better than people with schizoaffective disorder, and that people with schizoaffective disorder function better than those with schizophrenia, alone?"

Dr. Mitchell thought for a moment before she answered.

"No, Hannah, I wouldn't agree with that statement. The seriousness of the diagnosis doesn't affect productivity. A person's insight into their illness is what really affects how they are able to function."

"What do you mean?"

"Okay. Let's say a person has diabetes. They can feel their sugar dropping. Their symptoms are telling them something, so they take care of it. Maybe they take some medicine, or they eat something that will help their sugar to return to normal. The point is, they look at their disease outside of themselves and make decisions to help take care of their symptoms."

"In the same way, a person with a mental illness has to look at their symptoms as a disease separate from the individual. I know this approach is hard to do because it's the brain being affected with these negative symptoms. But if a person feels manic or depressed or is hearing voices, then they must act on those symptoms and take care of them, either by calling their doctor to change their medicine, by taking the necessary medicine at that time, or by getting in touch with their therapist. The point is, a person with a mental illness who has insight will not act on negative thoughts or delusions because they know that it is their disease acting up, not themselves."

Dr. Mitchell paused for a moment.

"Do you understand, Hannah?"

"I think so. Do I have this insight?"

"Yes. In the past, you have contacted me when your illness started acting up. That shows insight."

"Okay, good. Thanks."

"You're welcome."

Hannah got up out of her chair to leave.

"Take care," said Dr. Mitchell.

"Thanks. You too." Hannah exited the room, feeling refreshed and good about herself, a typical response to a visit with Dr. Mitchell.

She reentered her group therapy room in the middle of an interesting discussion, but before Hannah heard more of it, she was confronted by Ms. Jordan.

"How'd it go with the doctor, Hannah?" asked Ms. Jordan, addressing her as she walked in the room.

"It went good."

"Good. Did you find out about your medicine?"

"Yes. One of the nurses in the hospital made a mistake."

"Okay. Do you have your medicine now?"

"Yes. I got it yesterday afternoon after class."

"Good. That's good. We're talking about how to avoid a relapse. Can you think of a coping skill that would help keep you from going backwards in your recovery?"

"Umm. I really like listening to music and meditating on peaceful scenes in my mind. I also like praying scripture back to God."

"Good. Actually, great. That's great."

Hannah looked at the other answers on the board, under the title, "Coping Skills." Listed were the words "watching TV," "reading," "exercise and stretching," "baking and cooking," "visiting with friends," "doing artwork," "being in nature," and "breathing exercises." Ms. Jordan added Hannah's "listening to music," "meditation," and "prayer" to the list.

Hannah quickly pulled out her journal and wrote down all the words listed on the board. At that moment, she determined to incorporate most of those coping skills into her life because the last thing she wanted was a relapse. Perpetual, or at least initial, sanity was in her sights.

The day passed quickly, and Hannah found herself eventually seated in the van headed back to The Refuge. When she walked in the door, Ms. Rosie greeted her.

"Hey, Hannah," she said.

"Yes, ma'am?"

"One of the women in the house, Georgie, has moved out. I have a bed for you upstairs. You will be staying in the room with Beth. You have your own closet space. Just move your stuff in there."

"Okay, great, thanks," said Hannah.

Hannah was very grateful that she had her own bed now. She immediately headed upstairs to move her locker and clothes into her new space. As she carried her belongings into her new room, she spoke to Beth, who was seated in the room on her own bed. Beth was a woman in her fifties with long, jet black hair and an awkward gait.

"Hi, you're Beth?"

"Yes."

"I'm Hannah. I'm your new roommate."

"Oh, okay. Ms. Rosie told you to come in here?"

"Yeah."

Hannah immediately noticed that Beth spoke in an unusual, confusing way, and Hannah had trouble under-standing her. Beth responded with an awkward comment.

"Well, I don't rightly know how Ms. Rosie made the decision for you to come in here, but I guess it's all right with me, not that I have any say about it."

"Okay. I'm not a troublemaker, so you don't have to worry about me," said Hannah.

"Well, to tell you the truth, I don't rightly know how I got here, except to say that my boyfriend and I weren't getting along; and I came here without a stitch of clothes to my name, except for the clothes on my back."

"Uh huh."

"And to tell you the truth, I wasn't sure what he said to me at the time that didn't make sense to me; but I know that after he said what he did, it didn't ring true with me. And that's all I have to say about that."

"I'm sorry, but I don't understand what you're talking about," replied Hannah.

"Well, I don't rightly know if he meant it, but we discussed it at length; and I made sure he told the truth, as far as I can say. To tell you the truth, I don't think he meant it at all."

"You don't know if he meant what?"

Beth continued speaking as if she did not hear Hannah's question.

"And I told him it wasn't right what he said, but he seemed determined to let me know how he felt about it."

"You're kind of talking in riddles, and I'm not following what you are saying," said Hannah.

Beth kept talking. "Well, to tell you the truth, I can't say whether he meant it or not; but as long as I was around, he didn't say anything more about the subject."

After listening to Beth for about thirty minutes, Hannah decided to give up trying to understand exactly what her new roommate was saying. While Beth gave out her confusing discourse, Hannah vaguely listened and quit responding, since Beth didn't seem to be talking directly to Hannah anyway.

To escape the babble, Hannah went downstairs and sat in the dining room. Torrie was sitting at the kitchen table coloring in a coloring book.

"Hi," said Hannah.

"Oh, hi," said Torrie.

"Mind if I sit here?"

"Oh, no. That's fine."

Hannah sat down and watched Torrie color.

"Did you know that I lived with Indians in the 1800s?" asked Torrie.

Hannah looked into Torrie's eyes. She was dead serious.

"Uh, no. You did?"

"Yeah. I lived with a tribe, and they taught me how to hunt and fish and cook."

Hannah was determined to be kind, even though she knew Torrie was delusional.

"Really?" asked Hannah. "What was that like?"

"It was a hard life. A really hard life."

"I can imagine."

Sitting at the table, Hannah realized that the people in the group home needed friendship, just like Hannah did. She decided to be a friend to the people around her and to be as positive as she could about her situation. What choice did she have? She could be negative and pessimistic or positive and hopeful. She chose the latter.

For now, her station in life was in limbo. She didn't know how long she was going to be in the group home, and she felt conflicted about that reality. She felt so out of sorts because her life was marked by predictable seasons—until now. She went to school for twelve years and graduated from high school. She went to college and got her degree. She started looking for a job. Even when she couldn't work, she went back to school or volunteered somewhere. She seemed to always know what her next step would be, but now, her future was so uncertain that she could hardly cope. All she knew was that she would be in the group home for a certain amount of time, although she didn't even know how long that would be. She would eventually live somewhere else, hopefully in an apartment either in Houston or in her hometown, but she didn't know where she would end up, exactly.

The only way to survive living in the unknown was to live in the moment and lean on her faith. She purposed to live in the present and take things one step at a time. She also leaned on God and trusted that He would provide for her future as He already had when she was in inpatient care. As she focused on her recovery, she sought after God with all her heart. She meditated on scripture in her prayer book regularly and diligently. She prayed those scriptures as prayers back to God, and He gradually became her source for sustenance. She prayed for her future and asked for God's blessing on it. So, for the most part, Hannah tried to be okay with her situation, for now.

7

Sophia

HANNAH WAS MEETING so many different people at The Refuge. Along with Beth, her roommate, and her housemates, Torrie, Amanda, Daphney, and Carla, she also met a young woman in her twenties who lived in one of the other bedrooms upstairs. Her name was Sophia. Sophia walked into the den one afternoon while Hannah was sitting there, reading her prayer book.

"Hey, how's it going?" Hannah greeted Sophia, who was fresh from a shower, wearing her pajamas.

"I'm sad," replied Sophia, sitting down on the couch next to Hannah. She was amazingly transparent for never having spoken to Hannah before.

Hannah immediately engaged. "How come?"

"I miss my boyfriend."

"Where's your boyfriend?"

"Back in my hometown." Sophia fiddled with a lock of her black-brown hair.

"What's his name?"

"Eduardo." She gave a broad smile of very white teeth.

"How old is he?"

"He's my age. Twenty."

"When was the last time you saw him?"

"Last week. I really miss him. I really love him." Sophia looked down at her hands and sighed.

"How did he get here?"

"Took the bus."

They talked for an hour. Hannah learned a great deal about Sophia and her present situation. She was a product of the foster care system and suffered from an anxiety disorder. Now, she had a legal guardian who was also a social worker who looked after Sophia and her needs while she stayed in the group home. Sophia was in that early twenties mode, a time in life when she desperately wanted to be on her own for the first time, make all of her own decisions, choose her own path in life, and live life to the fullest. Sophia felt trapped in the group home and wanted out.

"I want my own apartment, and I want to live with my boyfriend," she told Hannah.

"How would you pay your bills?" asked Hannah.

"With my disability check. I'm also going to go to school and study to become a nurse."

"Really? That's cool."

"Yeah. I've wanted to be a nurse since I was little."

"That's good."

"And I want to have a family of my own."

"You mean kids?" asked Hannah.

"Yeah. Lots of kids."

"I bet you would make a great mom."

"I want to be the mom I never had."

"You didn't like your foster parents?"

"I never really had time to get to know them. The courts kept moving me around. I kept going from one foster family to another in the city where I lived."

"That's rough."

"Yeah."

The two women stopped talking for a moment, long enough for Hannah to look down at her prayer book. Sophia noticed the book in Hannah's hands.

"Is that a Bible?"

"No, it's a prayer book. It has verses from the Bible that are prayers back to God."

"I wish I had a Bible." Tears filled Sophia's eyes.

Hannah felt deep compassion for her.

"I have an extra Bible you can have."

"Really?"

"Sure. Come upstairs."

Hannah took the lead and went upstairs with Sophia behind her. She opened her footlocker in her room and pulled out a small, thin, leather Bible.

"Here. It's yours." Hannah extended the gift to Sophia.

"Thanks." Sophia took the book, walked into her room, and lay down on her bed, flipping through the pages.

Hannah lay down on her own bed, thinking deeply about where she was in life. She was just short of being homeless. Her parents would never turn their backs on her, and she would never end up on the streets, though she felt she was one step away from being a desperate beggar.

Even now, begging was rampant in the group home and in outpatient therapy. Spare change or cigarettes was easily given away by anyone who had a heart. If Hannah really couldn't part with a few quarters, she would gently say, "I can't give it to you; I need it." Whoever was asking for the handout would generally accept her reason and move on.

Cigarettes ran scarce at the group home. Most of the residents at The Refuge in the women's and men's homes were on disability and received government checks every month. The bulk of those payments covered most of the allowance for the group home, which included rent, utilities, and food. Not much money was left over, which left many people scavenging for handouts from anyone else to pay for snacks, cigarettes, or minutes for their phone.

Colt had the habit of asking Hannah for a quarter every day. He always wanted a soda he couldn't afford.

"Can I borrow some change?" he asked Hannah on one of their breaks at the outpatient program.

Hannah smiled. "Sure." She handed over the silver coins.

They were on break after breakfast, and Colt and Hannah sat in the lobby and talked for a while before it was time to go back into group.

"So why are you here?" asked Colt.

"Oh, I got really stressed out from working so hard and started hearing voices, so I went into the main hospital last month. After my meds pulled me out of a psychosis, I came here."

"I hear voices sometimes, too, when I'm having an episode."

"Really?"

"Yeah. I'm diagnosed with schizoaffective disorder," said Colt.

"Really? Me too. Is that how you ended up here?"

"I went hunting with some friends, and I thought I saw this man pointing a gun at me, so I shot at him, but then suddenly he wasn't there at all. I was real confused. I shot my gun close to one of the guys I was with and almost hit him. Well, he pressed charges because he thought I was mad at him and shot at him out of meanness. I got jail time and then probation. So, the judge sent me to this program."

"So, you mean this person that you thought you saw pointing a gun at you was a hallucination?"

"Yeah. I wasn't trying to hurt anybody. Now everybody thinks I'm crazy."

"I don't think you're crazy," said Hannah.

"You don't?"

"No. I think you have a lot of good things to say in group."

"Thanks."

"You're welcome."

"Do you understand our diagnosis?" asked Colt.

"Well, I know it has traits of both bipolar disorder and schizophrenia, with mainly hallucinations and delusions in a psychosis. I usually only have symptoms when I'm having an episode. I know it is hard to understand."

"Oh, yeah. It is definitely hard to understand," said Colt.

"Insanity is horrible," said Hannah.

"Yeah. I'd give anything to be a whole person again."

"Me too. I know my brain needs special care," said Hannah. "These erratic neurotransmitters in my brain are out of whack and unbalanced. I can handle that I'm bipolar, but I have a hard time admitting that I have features of schizophrenia along with it. Schizophrenia is such a scary word in our society, and I don't want people to be afraid of me. And they don't have to be. If I'm in an episode with my illness, I'm usually not out in public. I'm usually holed up in my room or in the hospital."

"Yeah, same with me," said Colt.

"I think schizophrenia is a highly misunderstood illness," said Hannah. "It's often episodic. At least that's how it happens with me—in episodes or seasons. And medication can help an ill person become a very high-functioning individual."

"Oh, yeah, I agree with you there," said Colt.

Hannah looked into Colt's eyes and felt a strong connection with him. She had never felt such helpful peer support in all the years that she had battled with her illness. She felt encouraged for the first time since her symptoms began to show up years ago. A light shone through Colt's beautiful eyes and touched a part of Hannah that no one had ever reached before. Someone understood her—and that meant everything.

"Time for group," Ms. Jordan called. She was rounding up the troops for another round of lessons about life. Hannah and Colt headed back to the meeting room, both feeling refreshed.

"Good talking with you," said Hannah.

"You too," said Colt.

After everyone took their seats and settled down, Mr. Kingsley, the outpatient director, entered the room. A large man, he was built like an NFL linebacker and spoke with a rough, throaty voice to go with his pumped-up physique.

"Everyone, please welcome Mr. Kingsley, our director, to the group. He has something he'd like to talk with you about," said Ms. Jordan.

Kingsley spoke with authority. He raised his voice when he began to talk. "Thanks for the opportunity to speak to you. I have a question. Is this program named dating-dot-com? Is this a place for you to meet your future husband or wife? Is this place prime real estate for a pick-up?"

The group was silent. Hannah felt her face getting hot.

Kingsley continued. "The answer to my questions is an emphatic 'No.' We have a rule that no one is allowed to develop personal relationships outside of group with anyone else that attends our program. Does anyone know why?"

More silence filled the room.

"We have this rule because we have found that personal involvement between patients outside of group hampers your psychological growth and recovery while you are here."

Hannah looked over at Colt, her mind racing.

"We have cameras all around this place for your protection. If there is any physical contact between clients, then we will know about it."

A huge question entered Hannah's mind. Did they just observe her and Colt talking in the lobby? All they were doing was talking. No physical contact occurred. Was Mr. Kingsley talking about her and Colt? She had spoken once before with Colt during breakfast. Were they being watched?

"We want the best for all of you. Thank you for your cooperation. Ms. Jordan, I will now hand the group back over to you."

Hannah felt so good about her conversations with Colt that she convinced herself that Mr. Kingsley couldn't possibly be talking about her or Colt, although what they discussed was indeed personal. She purposed in her heart to be careful with how she acted towards Colt while in the program. That resolution lasted about five minutes. Even though she felt conflicted about her feelings for Colt, Hannah sat next to him on the van because she wanted to be near him. For some reason, she felt safe with him, though she determined not to have any physical contact with him. Without knowing her feelings, Colt showed respect to her by honoring her space, which made her like him even more.

Arriving at the group home, Hannah's thoughts of Colt were immediately bombarded. Just as she walked in the front door, she saw Carla's right fist connect with Ms.

Rosie's left eyebrow, causing blood to spew from Ms. Rosie's face. Carla's ring on her fist cut Ms. Rosie's skin.

"Stop, Carla, stop!" yelled Ms. Rosie. Carla ran from the house to the back patio outside. Ms. Rosie grabbed a towel from the kitchen to stop the blood from pouring from her face. She pulled out her cell phone and called the police.

"I need the police to come and get one of my residents. She just assaulted me," she said to the 911 operator.

Less than five minutes later, a sharp rap was heard at the door. Two police officers stood at the door, talking with Ms. Rosie, who was holding the towel against her bloody face.

"Come in. She's in the back."

"Do you want to press charges?" asked one of the officers.

"Yes, but I want you to see if you can take her to the inpatient hospital instead of jail. She's out here outside."

The two policemen followed Ms. Rosie to the back of the house and reentered with Carla in handcuffs.

Carla didn't say a word, but she showed that familiar creepy smile on her face.

They exited the house and left in a patrol car.

"I can't have that nonsense in my house. I just can't," said Ms. Rosie, still doctoring her face. "I have to go to the ER to get stitches. You guys hang tight here with Mr. Paul, okay?"

"Yes, ma'am," the women answered in unison.

All the women—Hannah, Torrie, Beth, Daphney, Amanda, and Sophia—congregated in the den during all the commotion. After Carla exited the house, they sat on a large sectional couch in the den and watched TV.

"Now, maybe we'll have some peace and quiet around the house," said Torrie.

"No kidding," said Daphney.

Truthfully, harmony seemed to enter the house just as soon as Carla left it. Even Amanda was in good spirits. The women relaxed and watched the evening news while they waited for dinner. Mr. Paul was preparing a dish of red beans and rice, and the women seemed content to wait for the good cooking. In the midst of the drama, Ms. Rosie's strong resolve to keep the peace in the house was a comfort to the women, and Hannah was grateful.

After dinner, Hannah rested in the den until it was time to go to bed. She owned a book full of peaceful nature photos that she kept near her to look through if she needed to focus on good thoughts. While Hannah was reading, Sophia padded into the room in her slippers and plopped down on the sofa next to Hannah.

"How long you been here?" Sophia asked Hannah.

Hannah thought a moment. "I've been here about a month. What about you?"

"Two months."

"How's it going?"

"Oh, I wish I could see my boyfriend. I miss him so much."

"Where were you before you came here?"

"I was in another group home, but it wasn't safe. An older girl was beating up on me. And a couple of the guys wanted to have sex with me, but I didn't want to. My social worker moved me here."

"How long have you and your boyfriend been dating?"

"A year."

"Is he the one?" asked Hannah.

"What do you mean?"

"Do you think you will get married?"

"He gave me a promise ring."

"Well, that's hopeful."

Sophia smiled.

"Well, I'm going to bed," said Hannah.

"Yeah, me too."

They trudged upstairs and went to their respective rooms.

"Night, Sophia," said Hannah.

"Night," she replied.

Another day of outpatient therapy and group home life was ending, and Hannah thought about her progress in the program. She knew she would have to wait some time before she reached full recovery, but she was beginning to carry herself with the smallest bit of confidence. She hoped this confidence would gradually grow inside of her so she could be fully independent.

Hannah thought about Colt and how careful she needed to be in her relationship with him. By general standards, she was a rule keeper. She didn't want to cause any trouble with Mr. Kingsley by having a friendship with

Colt, but she also wanted to encourage and support Colt as much as she could. Perhaps she could find a sustainable middle ground. As always, she overanalyzed the situation until she finally nodded off and fell asleep for the night.

IN THE MIDDLE of the night, Hannah was aroused from her slumber by the sound of choking in the bathroom. Hannah climbed out of bed, quietly knocked on the closed bathroom door, and pushed the door open slightly. She noticed that Sophia was throwing up.

"You okay, Sophia?" asked Hannah.

"I'm sick," she said.

"Can I come in?"

"Yeah."

Hannah entered the dimly lit bathroom, fished a washcloth out of the bathroom cabinet, and ran cool water over it. Then she handed it to Sophia, who wiped her face and sighed deeply.

"Thanks," said Sophia.

"No problem. What did you eat?"

"Same as you. Red beans and rice."

"Did you eat too much?"

"No. I think I'm pregnant."

"Oh, okay." Hannah paused a moment. "Is this the first time you've thrown up?"

"No, I started getting sick yesterday morning."

"Okay. You better ask the nurse tomorrow to give you a pregnancy test."

"Yeah."

"Do you want me to stay with you?"

"No, I'm okay. Thanks."

Hannah crept back to her bedroom and slid back under the covers of her bed. Thoughts raced through her mind. How would Sophia care for a baby in the group home? She tried to go back to sleep, but she struggled to relax. Her day had been long and eventful. She hoped she could go to sleep soon. Each day was so full of new things, and she wanted to get some rest for the one approaching.

8

Choices

THE FIRST THING on Hannah's mind the next morning was Sophia's sickness, due to a possible pregnancy. She wondered how Sophia would survive with a child in the situation she was in. As Hannah went downstairs for breakfast, she noticed that some lights were flashing in front of the men's house across the street.

"Heard someone got busted for drugs," said Torrie, who was seated at the kitchen table, sipping her coffee.

"Really?" said Hannah.

"Yeah," said Torrie, turning her head to look outside the curtains of the front window at the police car parked out front.

AFTER HANNAH ARRIVED at outpatient group therapy, Ms. Jordan introduced a new topic.

"Why do we make bad choices?" she asked the group.

"Convenience," answered Sydney, as he pulled at the hairs of his long goatee.

"Okay." She wrote his answer on the board. "Anybody else?"

"Being hasty," said Sam, running his nervous fingers through his hair.

"Not controlling your anger," said Colt, smacking on a fresh piece of bubble gum.

"Okay, good. Give me some more." She kept writing.

"Avoiding stress," said Andrea.

"Okay, yeah. What else?"

"Receiving bad information," said Hannah. "Being misinformed."

"What do you mean?" asked Ms. Jordan.

"Making a decision based on some false information somebody gives you."

"Okay, good. What else?"

"Listening to others' bad influence," said Martha.

"Okay, good. Bad peer pressure can be very detrimental. How about good choices? How do we make good choices?"

Colt spoke first. "I think we make good choices if we carefully weigh our options."

"That's a good one," said Ms. Jordan.

Hannah raised her hand.

"Yes, Hannah?"

"Taking time to think about it and even sleep on it."

"Okay, good. Anybody else?" There was a pause.

"What about talking to people you trust before making a good choice?" asked Ms. Jordan.

A few heads nodded.

"Let's go back to bad choices. What are some examples of bad choices?"

"Speeding," said Colt.

"Smokin' weed," said Sydney.

"Sleeping around," said Andrea.

"Okay, good. What can happen if we speed or take illegal drugs or act promiscuously? What can happen as a result of these choices?"

"If you speed, you could get a ticket or get in a wreck," said Colt.

"Right," said Ms. Jordan. "Or someone could get seriously hurt. What about doing drugs, how will that hurt you?"

"If you smoke dope, it can mess up your mind or get you arrested," said Sydney.

"Okay. Good thoughts. What about promiscuity? What can happen to you if you sleep with a lot of people?"

"You can get diseases," said Sydney.

"Right. What else?"

"You could get pregnant when you don't want to," said Hannah, who was thinking about Sophia.

"Good. These answers are good points. All very good thoughts. How can we know we are making the right choices?"

"I guess if you know the outcome will be good, then it means you are about to make a good choice," said Hannah.

"Okay. What are some good outcomes?"

"If you eat right, you will feel better and look better," said Martha.

"That's right. Anybody else?"

"If I am polite when I ask a question, then I will get a nice response back," said Sam.

"Yes, that may be true, if the person you are talking with is also polite," said Ms. Jordan.

"Sometimes I hear voices through the radio, and they are not polite," said Sam.

"What do the voices say?"

"They say that I'm ugly and don't belong here."

"Is that true?"

"I don't know if it's true or not. I just know that I want those voices to stop."

"Okay. How can you make a good choice about the voices you hear on the radio?"

"Umm. Tell them to shut up?"

"Well, that's one choice. What is a better choice? Can anyone help Sam with this one?"

"You can just turn off the radio or change the station," said Colt.

"Yes, that's good. What else?"

"You can write good, positive thoughts about yourself in your journal and repeat them in your mind to fight what the voices are saying about you," said Hannah.

"Absolutely. Do you do that sometimes, Hannah?"

"Yes, ma'am, sometimes I do."

"What do you write?"

"I am a good person. I am kind. I am loving. Stuff like that."

"Okay. Does anybody else write good stuff about themselves in their journal?"

Silence filled the room.

"Oh, I see. Okay. We are going to turn this topic into a project right now. I am going to hand you a piece of paper, and I want you to write down five things that are positive about yourself, and we'll see how you do."

Ms. Jordan passed out the paper to the six patients. Colt, Sydney, Sam, Hannah, Martha, and Andrea all eagerly got to work. Pencils scribbling on paper was the only sound heard for several minutes.

"When you are finished, put your pencils down," said Ms. Jordan.

After several more minutes, Andrea was still writing— she was the last one in the group still working on the project.

"Andrea, are you finished?"

"No, ma'am. I can only think of three."

"Okay, that's fine. Who would like to share their positive statements?"

"I will," said Sydney, raising his hand.

"Okay, go ahead."

"I am good-looking. I am considerate. I am strong. I am determined. I am helpful."

"Okay. Those are all very good. Thank you, Sydney. Who's next?"

"I'll go," said Colt. "I'm a good hunter. I am a good friend. I'm a good cook. I'm a good athlete. I'm a good fisherman."

"Thank you, Colt. What's your favorite meal to cook?"

"Steak and baked potatoes."

"Sounds good. Okay, who wants to share their statements?"

"I will," said Hannah. "I am positive. I am loved. I am valued. I am cherished. I am an encourager."

"Okay, that's good stuff. Does anyone else want to share?"

"I do," said Martha.

"Okay, go ahead."

"I am wise. I am giving. I am smart. I am good. I am pretty."

"That's great, Martha. Anyone else?"

No one raised their hands. The room became very quiet. Obviously, Andrea and Sam wanted to keep their answers to themselves.

"Okay, it's time to take a break. Good work, you guys."

The six patients filtered out of the room and went to different areas in the building to relax. Hannah made her way to the lobby. Colt followed her.

"Hey, Hannah," he called to her as she sat down in a chair next to the door.

"Hey," Hannah responded.

"I liked what you said about yourself in group."

"Oh, thanks. You too." She paused. "You used to be an athlete? I used to be an athlete."

"Really? Are you still one?"

"No." Hannah looked down at her hands. "I started taking medicine that made me gain weight. Then I couldn't compete anymore."

"What did you do?"

"I played soccer," said Hannah.

"Really? That's cool."

"What kind of sports did you play?" asked Hannah.

"I ran track and played wide receiver in football," he said.

As Colt talked, Hannah particularly noticed his well-rounded physique, his bulging biceps, his tight chest. She quit listening to what he was saying.

"Hannah?"

"Yes?" She snapped back to attention, realizing that she had become distracted.

"Are you okay?"

She cleared her throat. "Uh, yeah, why?"

"You just drifted off to some kind of never-never land," he laughed.

"Oh," she chuckled. "Sorry. I got distracted."

She wondered if Colt knew she found him so attractive. At the same time, she wondered how he felt about her.

"I'll catch you later," said Colt.

"Okay," she said.

As Colt walked away, Hannah realized that she was beginning to care deeply about some of the people around her. She wanted to get to know Colt better. She worried about Sophia and her possible pregnancy. She wondered why Beth, her roommate, never made any sense. She wondered if Torrie, her housemate, was really a former detective. Hannah also wished that Amanda and Daphney would stop fighting and get along better. She also wished that she could have a better relationship with them. She felt sad for Andrea in her group because she seemed so lost and painfully shy. She wished that Sam didn't hear voices in the radio. She wondered how Ms. Rosie managed to keep her two houses running with all the different people living there and with all the issues she had to deal with.

Hannah kept these thoughts to herself. These people all around her made her feel secure, like she finally belonged, for once in all the years that she had struggled with her illness. These were everyday people with mental illnesses of some sort, and she identified with them. She understood them. She could relate to them. Their illnesses interrupted normal life for them. The heartbreak of mental instability knocked them off course from a healthy life. Now they needed to figure out how to be as stable as possible, even with a debilitating illness, and how to make good choices to maintain their health.

Hannah also began to think about her present situation. She was a twenty-something woman living in a group home. She had a crush on a guy who almost shot someone. She was gaining about seven pounds a week. Her father was on a serious health decline, and she was very concerned about him.

Hannah once again began to entertain worried thoughts about her future. When she got too much into her head, she would worry about what lay ahead. She didn't know how long she would be in the outpatient program or at The Refuge group home. Her only solace was to live life in the present—and that meant the absolute present: not day by day, not hour by hour, but second by second. Breathe in, breathe out, left foot, right foot, breathe in, breathe out, left foot, right foot. She needed to take one step at a time. She had to concentrate this way and face life with such simplicity because she would simply deteriorate into a ball of despair if she wondered too much about her future. The future was too big, too scary, and frankly, too uncertain. All she knew was that she had a big God who was on her side, and she took comfort in knowing He had everything under control. Thankfully, someone did.

Her mind eventually drifted to the most important thought she could presently have, and that was how she was ever going to get back home and be independent. She decided to make a good choice and start setting some goals, with going home as a goal.

At the end of the day at outpatient while she waited for the van to take her back to The Refuge, Hannah scribbled furiously in her journal, escaping into a deep focus. She considered her behavior and tried to think about how to possibly overcome her illness by making some good choices. She wrote down seven priorities that she thought she needed to concentrate on if she was going to continue to get better.

First, she needed to keep seeking God and exercising her faith. Prayer, bible study, meditating on scripture, and regular worship would help her tremendously. She also needed to get involved in a church wherever she ended up. Support from the people she loved in a church community was something she would need if she aimed to gain some independence from the group home.

Second, she needed to take her meds religiously. That would be a good choice. She thought about the last several years of her illness and how the stability of her mind tended to fluctuate with her meds. Years ago, when first medicated heavily, she weaned herself off her meds on her own when she began to feel better. Making that kind of move is typical and common for a person with a new mental illness; but, in the end, it can be a very dangerous decision. In the situation of her chronic illness, symptoms of the illness eventually resurfaced without proper medication. So, of utmost importance was medication management. She would continue working with her doctor to keep her levels balanced and would hope for the best.

Third, she needed to get on a regular sleep pattern and stick to the routine. Her most recent manic episode had flourished into an obsessive workaholic madness that led to sleepless nights and long hours of intense mental activity. She loved to be focused and thorough in whatever she did, but her body and brain just couldn't sustain that level of pressure for very long. She made a goal to consistently be in bed between ten and twelve p.m. She usually woke up around six a.m. at the group home. If she eventually got back to her hometown, she would train herself to wake up later at eight a.m. *That's a good eight to ten hours of sleep*, she thought. She really needed that much sleep to function well. Getting enough sleep was a good choice.

Her next priority was meditation. She needed to keep her focus on good things, good memories, beautiful nature scenes, positive sayings, and positive self-talk. She also needed to keep reading her prayer book and meditate on good thoughts towards God. She was never so con-scientious about maintaining healthy thoughts until this time in her life. The process of thinking well and meditating on good things had helped to get her out of the inpatient hospital and surely would help her to stay out.

Next, she needed to work on her food intake. She had developed a big appetite as a result of her meds. She had gained weight very rapidly and had quickly become overweight. Eating in a healthy way was one of her biggest struggles because everything she ate tasted so good, and she never really felt full until after she had overeaten. She decided to keep a food journal or diary to keep track of exactly what she was eating every day. Maybe that would help her keep the carbs down. If she felt better physically, she would feel better mentally.

For her sixth goal, she realized that if she was going to stay productive, she needed to get involved in volunteer work. In the past, she had freelanced for a newspaper. She reasoned that maybe she could do that again. Even though she didn't get paid for it, she was still excited about seeing her articles in print. She also thought that she might help to socialize the dogs that were at the local animal shelter. She had worked with some of these dogs before and working with canines was good therapy for her.

Exercise, goal number seven, was at the bottom of the list because she hated it so much. As an overweight woman, nothing was more tiring and discouraging than exercise. So why put it on the list? Maybe because every physician she ever talked with told her she needed to get her weight down and to try and do some exercise. So, she earnestly thought about trying to exercise, although she didn't know exactly how she was going to do it yet.

"What are you doing?" asked Colt, who walked up to her and interrupted her thoughts. He leaned over her shoulder and looked at the journal. "You look like you are writing an essay for an English test, all serious and everything."

"Oh," she smiled sheepishly. "I was just setting some goals."

"You are so intense."

"I know. I need help."

"No, no, I like that."

"Really?"

"Yeah. So many people around here don't care about anything. I've never met anyone as focused as you."

"And . . . you think that's a good thing?"

"Yeah, I do. Don't change a thing."

Hannah smiled.

They were interrupted by Nathan, the van driver. He didn't put up with slow movers. "All patients going to The Refuge load up now. The van is leaving," he called.

"That's our cue," said Colt.

Hannah put her journal back in her satchel and walked outside with the group. She was grateful for Colt. She was grateful for The Refuge. She was grateful for many things. She believed that God gave her this gift of gratitude. Gratitude literally kept her going, putting one foot in front of the other, pushing forward, keeping the faith, and having hope. She also was grateful that they talked about choices in outpatient. She thought she was on the road to making good choices for herself.

Nathan played a soulful station on the ride home. They rode back in silence, each person seeming to be lost in thought. Listening to the music, Hannah felt empowered. She hoped to be like the strong woman singing on the radio—brimming with potential, hopeful for the future, confident in herself, and open to good possibilities.

9

The Drama

WHEN SHE REACHED The Refuge, Hannah discovered a distressed Beth in her room, apparently shouting to no one in particular.

"You can't make me say what I don't want to say!" she shouted out towards the door.

Hannah reasoned that maybe Beth was yelling at Amanda in the next room, but she wasn't sure.

"You're full of bull if you ask me! You're no good, I tell you, no good!"

As usual, Hannah did not know what her roommate was talking about. She went downstairs in search of Ms. Rosie to see if she knew what was going on. She found the homeowner at the kitchen table filling out paperwork. Ms. Rosie looked up and saw Hannah, who had a puzzled look on her face.

"I don't know what's wrong with Beth, Ms. Rosie."

"I think Beth is having trouble, that's what's wrong."

Ms. Rosie organized her paperwork, put it all in a folder, and headed up the stairs.

"Beth, pack your things and get your I.D., I'm taking you to the hospital."

"She told me a lie, I tell you! A lie!"

"I don't know what you're talking about," said Ms. Rosie. "Now, pack your things, like I said, or go like you are. It's your choice."

Beth kept ranting while she grabbed some clothes and stuffed them in a bag.

"I told them to leave me alone!" she hollered.

"Come on, Beth, let's go," said Ms. Rosie.

Ms. Rosie picked up Beth's bag of belongings and marched downstairs. "Let's go, Beth, come on. They can help you with what you're upset about, in the hospital."

Beth trumped downstairs, following Ms. Rosie. She kept yelling on her way out the door. Hannah didn't understand what was wrong with Beth. She suspected that maybe she was hearing voices, and she was yelling at the voices she heard in her head.

After Beth and Ms. Rosie left, Hannah turned on The Brady Bunch and sat on her bed, relieved that she had the room to herself. Sophia knocked on the door to the room.

"Hey, Sophia," said Hannah.

"Hey. Looks like you got your own room."

"Yeah. At least for now."

"That's cool."

"How are you doing?" asked Hannah.

"I'm still feeling sick."

"Did you talk with the nurse? Did you get a pregnancy test?"

"No, not yet. The nurse is coming this afternoon."

"Did you tell your caseworker?"

"Yeah."

"What did she say?"

"She just said to take the test and wait and see what happens."

"Are you worried?"

"No. I think I would like to have a baby."

"Really?"

"Yeah."

"Oh, okay."

Hannah decided that the best she could do for Sophia was to encourage her and to love her like a friend. After they talked a few more minutes, Sophia left and went back to her room. Hannah lay on her bed and rested, trying to think good thoughts. She didn't know what to think about having a room to herself. She had progressed quite a bit from the original blow-up mattress, to now.

Quite abruptly, she heard the loud yell of Amanda's voice and the voice of some man she did not know, coming from downstairs. Hannah closed her door but left a crack open to see if she could hear the rather aggressive argument going on.

"Oh, yeah, so that's what you think, huh, Evan?"

"Mandy, be reasonable."

"Oh, reasonable. That's a fresh one. No one has been reasonable with me ever since I went into the hospital. Reasonable. Ha!"

"We are doing this for your own protection."

"Oh, great, just what I need, someone looking out for my own welfare. I'm thirty years old! I think I can take care of myself."

"But you know your thinking has been. . ."

"My thinking is fine. I had a concussion, okay. A concussion! I am not giving up my rights so you can feel good about how things are going. What about me? What about what I want?"

Just then Hannah heard Mr. Paul. He must have just walked in the door.

"All right, Amanda, nobody needs to know your whole business. If y'all are going to argue, take it outside on the patio."

Hannah heard Amanda and Evan's voices fade, but she could still hear them yelling outside her window. Hannah thought about their argument. She realized that one of the hardest things all the women wrestled with was their lack of independence. The thought of being so needy was quite demoralizing. Grown adults generally do not appreciate it when they must listen to other grown adults tell them what to do about their future.

Sophia knocked on Hannah's door.

"Come in," said Hannah.

"That's Amanda's brother."

"What's going on?"

"He wants her to sign over guardianship to him so he can help pay her bills."

"Why does he have to be her guardian?" asked Hannah.

"He's not allowed to mess with her bank account right now. He needs written permission. And she's not thinking straight."

"Oh."

The argument, now being heard from outside, escalated. They could hear Amanda yelling.

"Those are nice shoes you got there, Evan. Where'd you get the money for that, huh? Think I'm going to let you touch my money? Now that really would be crazy!"

Just then Torrie knocked on Hannah's door. Sophia opened it.

"Hey," said Hannah.

"Wow, they are really going at it, huh?" said Torrie.

"Sometimes having a guardian can be a good thing," said Hannah.

"Yeah, as long as you trust them. I think I'm going to let my parents be my guardians," said Torrie.

"I thought your parents didn't know where you were," said Hannah.

"What? Why do you say that?"

"Remember when you said you were in Witness Protection?"

"Oh, yeah. That. That was a delusion."

"Oh, okay," said Hannah. She changed the subject. "Is dinner almost ready?"

"Yeah. Having pork chops," said Sophia.

"Sounds good," said Hannah. *Thank goodness for the cooking*, Hannah thought.

Hannah stopped to think about Amanda for a few moments. She thought that deep down underneath all that anger was a whole bunch of fear—fear of the unknown, fear of being poor and homeless, fear of being out of control. It's a scary thing when someone else is calling the shots on your life. Trust must be there first.

Hannah was still well enough to make decisions on her own and that was a good thing, too. Since she was able to be decisive, Hannah decided that tomorrow she would call Michael about apartment hunting—at least that would be a start. The decision made her feel like she was moving towards independence, and she felt good about that.

THE WOMEN AT THE Refuge eventually settled in their beds for the evening, although the night was far from over. Hannah was near a dream-like sleep when Torrie knocked on her door.

"Hey, Hannah," she called softly.

Hannah awoke and answered the door.

"What's up?"

"There's some flashing lights in front of the men's house across the street again. I'm going over there to find out the scoop."

"Okay, be careful."

Hannah followed Torrie downstairs and looked out the window in front of the kitchen table. The flashing lights were coming from a fire truck. Several men stood outside by the truck. Hannah could see Torrie walking around talking to people. When she came back, she spoke to Hannah.

"Guess what?"

"What's going on?"

"They're checking out Mr. Paul. They think he may have had a stroke."

"Oh, no!" said Hannah. "What happened?"

"He was cleaning one of the men's bathrooms and felt one side of his body go numb. He sat down and had heart palpitations, and someone called 911."

"Is he okay, now?"

"I don't know. They are taking him to the ER. I'm going back to find out some more."

Torrie left again out the front door and headed to the flashing lights outside. Hannah watched through the window. A police car drove up with lights flashing. Though it was dark, the lights helped Hannah to see better. She saw a scuffle between some of the men and a fireman. The police jumped out of the car and broke up the altercation. Then she saw Torrie hurrying back to the women's home.

"What's going on now?" asked Hannah.

"You know Sydney?" asked Torrie, out of breath.

"Yeah."

"He just got in a fight with one of the firemen."

"About what?"

"I don't know, but he was sure mad."

"What's going to happen to Sydney?"

"The cops are taking him to the station. He's in the back seat of the police car right now."

Hannah felt bad for Sydney. She really liked him and liked having him in her outpatient therapy group.

"Wow, busy night," said Hannah.

"I know."

"Maybe Ms. Rosie will take us to see Mr. Paul tomorrow."

"You mean if he stays in the hospital?"

"Yeah," said Hannah.

"Oh, I doubt it. Ms. Rosie is pretty strict about everyone going to their centers," said Torrie.

"Why?" asked Hannah.

"I don't know. Because of insurance, I think."

"Oh."

Hannah admired Torrie. She didn't seem to be afraid of anything. She walked right in the middle of everything and found out what was going on. Hannah didn't feel secure enough to do that.

"Do you think Mr. Paul is okay?" asked Hannah.

"I don't know. I hope so," said Torrie.

"Me too. I really like him."

"Yeah, he's cool. He's a good cook, too."

The two women didn't speak for a few moments. They were taking in the weight of what was happening around them. When something happened at The Refuge that affected the atmosphere of the group home, the experience was hard to digest for a while. Everyone had to get used to the change. Change revealed the true instability of their environment. This lack of control threatened the sense of security they so desperately needed. These un-expected occurrences, however, caused the women to draw closer to each other for support.

Mr. Paul was a good man. He was stable, fair, and honest. Hannah didn't want him to leave. She felt safe when Mr. Paul was around.

Torrie spoke. "Well, how do you think Beth is doing?"

"I don't know. I think she was in a psychosis when she left here."

"Why do you say that?"

"I think she was yelling at voices she was hearing in her mind," said Hannah.

"How do you know?"

"Well, I don't know for sure, but the things she was saying make me think that she was feeling attacked by audio hallucinations."

"They probably are going to give her some tranquilizers to calm her down in the hospital," said Torrie.

"Yeah. She seems to be very angry and feeling a lot of pain and confusion."

"I know how that feels," said Torrie.

"Yeah. Me too."

Whenever Hannah had been in a psychosis in the main hospital, she was emotionally paralyzed. The voices tormented her so much that she couldn't function well. Hannah was convinced that being in a psychosis was one of the most unsettling and troubling experiences a person could go through. Trying to endure it was even excruciating. When she experienced a psychosis, she was overwhelmed by the feeling of being completely out of control of her mind. She would experience audio hallucinations, or hear voices, that interrupted the normal thought flow in her brain.

Many times, the audio hallucinations bombarded her brain so intensely that there was no relief from the constant barrage. Hannah had been in a psychosis for about three weeks while in the main hospital. She stayed there almost a month. The experience was unbearable.

Torrie asked a question that interrupted Hannah's thoughts.

"Have you ever been in a psychosis?"

"Yeah, I have," answered Hannah.

"What does a psychosis feel like to you?"

Hannah thought for a moment. She struggled to explain. She finally began to talk.

"When I am overcome with a psychosis, I feel like I am in two worlds. I live in one reality, which is the world or my environment; and I live in an alternate reality, which is in my mind. The first reality and the alternate reality enmesh a little bit, but they are really two different worlds. I get so consumed by the alternate reality in my mind, trying to survive within it, that I can't function properly in the first reality, in the world." She paused. "Does that make sense?"

"I guess so," answered Torrie. "Maybe that's what happens when I go into a psychosis, but I'm not sure."

"What do you think about?"

"Well, I have these weird thoughts that seem true at the time, but then later I realize they're not true."

"What is your diagnosis?"

"Schizoaffective disorder," said Torrie.

"That's what I have, too."

"How is schizoaffective disorder different from just schizophrenia?" asked Torrie.

"I think people with just schizophrenia don't have the mood swings we have," said Hannah.

"I hate my illness," said Torrie.

"Yeah. It's a brutal disease."

"It's exhausting to not be able to trust my own mind."

"Yeah, and you feel so unsteady and insecure when the illness is full blown. And I hate how some people treat me when I'm in a psychosis. They seem to think I can control my thoughts at that time, but I can't," said Hannah.

"So how do you cope with your illness?" asked Torrie.

"Well, aside from taking meds, I've been practicing meditation a lot since I went into the main hospital."

"What do you do when you meditate?"

"I picture something beautiful in my mind and really focus on that and concentrate on taking deep breaths while I am meditating," said Hannah.

"Oh. I ought to try that. What sort of things do you picture in your mind?" asked Torrie.

"I really like peaceful nature scenes. And then I have a few other relaxing scenes that I keep just for myself to think about. Make sure you have some that are just for you and no one else," said Hannah.

"Okay." Torrie paused. "Why?"

"Because it somehow makes you feel whole inside, you know—intact, secure, strong."

"Like there's a part of you that no one can touch."

"Right," said Hannah. "And something else really works for me, too. Prayer. That's a big one."

"I like to pray, too."

"I will say a prayer for you tonight," said Hannah.

"Okay. Thanks." She stood there for a moment.

"Well, I better go to bed. I'm tired," said Torrie.

"Yeah. Me, too. Night," said Hannah.

"Night."

Hannah curled up under her covers and began to pray for Torrie. She prayed that Torrie would recover quickly and get to go home soon. Hannah prayed that for herself, too. Then she nodded off to sleep, breathing deeply.

10

Relationships

THE NEXT MORNING, Hannah and Torrie talked over coffee while they waited for their rides.

"Sometimes I just want to run away, but I tried that already," said Torrie to Hannah.

"When did you try to run away?"

"About four months ago. I was sick for about a year. I was an agoraphobic and wouldn't leave my room for anything. Then one day, I got really scared, scared to be in the house. I ran out of my room and down the road of my neighborhood. I ran hard for a long time, about a mile down the road. A police car passed by me and pulled over. He asked me if I needed help. I told him I was running away. He offered to drive me to the hospital, so I went with him."

"I tried to run away once," said Hannah.

"Really?" asked Torrie.

"Yeah."

"What happened?"

"I started running down my street, shouting out for God to help me."

"Really?"

"Yeah, but I didn't go far. I walked back to the house because my mom was calling for me. I was really sick."

"Were you hearing voices?" asked Torrie.

"Yeah. And I was real fearful, agitated, confused."

"I feel that way too, when I'm sick."

Just then Hannah's van honked its horn, and the women changed gears from restful conversation to an urgent awareness that it was time for a new day.

"Have a great day," said Hannah.

"You, too," said Torrie.

Hannah walked outside toward the van, joining the other residents who were gathering around the van's door, like a flock of wayward geese.

Colt politely let the women pile in first, and then he and Sam entered the van. Sydney wasn't there. He was still in jail. Colt sat almost completely on a hump at the edge of the second seat, earning dibs that morning for selflessness. Hannah sat behind him, his wide back partially blocking her view of the road ahead. She longed to reach up and give him a shoulder massage, to make some kind of positive expression of her longing to be near him; but she knew that physical contact was out of the question.

Hannah focused on what she could see of the road. The lines stretching out in front of her seemed to signify her future in some way, a path laid straight before her, begging her to simply follow it as it came. She took deep breaths and held them to the count of four, and then she exhaled quietly. Good coping skills, along with her faith, were the ticket to recovery—from stress, loneliness, and most of all, recovery from insanity. Meds were necessary too, of course, but coping skills and mindfulness, or being present with her thoughts in the moment, helped her mind to be more stable.

Insanity was the tragedy that had once embraced all of them. While losing one's mind consists of a myriad of different delusions and inner voices, one thing remains the same—a lack of control of one's thoughts preoccupies the sufferer to the point of agonizing obsession. Hannah was convinced that being crazy drove her even crazier, literally.

For now, she focused on learning as much as she could from outpatient services. She hoped that the education she gained would lead to growth and stability and help her reach her ultimate goal of autonomy.

WHEN HANNAH AND the others got settled in their group therapy room for the day, the therapist began to speak.

"Today we are going to talk about relationships," said their therapist, after she wrote down their scores on the happiness scale and their goals for the day. "Good relationships. Bad relationships. I really want you guys to participate today. It's important. Andrea, I need you to wake up, sit up, and really focus."

Andrea yawned and sat up, blinking her eyes.

Ms. Jordan continued. "First, let's look at bad relationships. What are signs of unhealthy relationships?"

The group listened attentively and began to answer, all at once, speaking over each other.

"Lying, cheating," said Martha.

"Betrayal," said Sam.

"Disrespect," said Colt.

"Not being a good listener," said Hannah.

"Co-dependency," said Andrea.

"Okay. Those are some really good answers," said Ms. Jordan, who was writing furiously on the board. Their immediate participation was unusual. Obviously, this subject was a hot topic. Ms. Jordan spoke again.

"What about good relationships? What are signs of healthy relationships?"

Hannah glanced over at Colt and thought for a second.

"Trust, loyalty, and respect," said Hannah.

"Good, Hannah. Anybody else?"

"Honesty and openness," said Colt.

Hannah and Colt's eyes met, and they both smiled.

"Okay, good," said Ms. Jordan. "What is the one crucial element that determines whether you end up in a good relationship or a bad relationship?"

The group was silent.

"Anybody have a guess?"

Still no answers came forward.

"Okay, I'll tell you. Developing relationships is all about choices. It's a matter of making good choices with a wise mind. Looking at a person's character, seeing how they act in different situations, and making good choices about how you want to interact with that person is key to finding a healthy relationship."

Hannah thought for a minute. She wondered how she and Colt fit into the situation. She thought she would be making a good choice of dating him if the program allowed it. He was a gentleman. He was kind. He was attractive. However, she couldn't help but consider the reason why he was there. He had almost killed someone in the middle of a hallucination. Could she ever feel safe with him? Her thoughts about the matter made her feel like a bigot, like she was judging him based on what he did in the middle of a psychotic episode rather than based on his real character. She didn't think Colt would have shot his gun if he had been in his right mind.

Ms. Jordan interrupted Hannah's thoughts.

"Okay. There's one more thing to think about. You should use caution when developing relationships. I don't mean that you should act out of fear, but you should definitely guard your heart."

"What does that mean?" asked Andrea.

"That means that you don't just trust your heart with anybody that comes along. Get to know what the person is about before you truly share your heart with them. Now I want you guys to help me out with another angle to this topic. What types of behavior in another person do you want to avoid in a relationship?"

Hannah spoke immediately. "If they talk about other people behind their backs, then they will probably do the same to you."

"Good point, Hannah. Anybody else?"

"If a girl you like flirts with everybody, then she's probably not the one for you," said Colt.

"Good, Colt."

Sam spoke. "If you know that a person steals from other people, like money or cigarettes, then you should stay away from them."

"That's true, Sam. That's a very good point. Martha? Andrea? Any thoughts about bad behavior in another person?"

"If someone doesn't keep a small promise, how can you trust them to keep bigger promises?" asked Martha.

"True. True. Good," said Ms. Jordan.

"I like people who really listen to me," said Andrea with unusual clarity.

"Yes. That's good. People who listen well show that they care about you," said Ms. Jordan. "Now I want to talk about one more thing that might help you in relationships. In a dating relationship, understanding each other's needs is important. I have read that guys need respect, and women need love. If you can remember that, you may have less problems along the way."

Hannah thought about Ms. Jordan's last comment. Disrespect was something Colt had mentioned earlier when they were discussing unhealthy relationships, which means that respect was not only important with guys in general, but also with Colt in particular. She purposed in her heart to be very respectful to him when they were together.

After their talk about relationships, Ms. Jordan dismissed the group for a break. Hannah decided that she needed to talk to Mr. Kingsley. She walked down the hall and knocked on Mr. Kingsley's door.

"Come in," he answered.

He was a kind, assertive man, intent on helping his clients by empowering them to be independent.

"Hi, Mr. Kingsley. I was wondering if I could talk to you for a minute."

"Sure. Have a seat."

"I need to start looking at apartments in my hometown. If I find a way to get home, will you allow me to miss the program for a few days at a time?"

"Yes, you can do that, if it's okay with your medical insurance. You ready to move on?"

"Yes, sir. I don't mind the group home as a temporary placement, but I don't want to live there forever. It's just a pit stop, you know?"

"Oh, sure, I understand. This may be a good step for you."

"I hope so," said Hannah. "Thanks, Mr. Kingsley."

"You're welcome." He stretched out his hand.

Hannah shook his gentle, strong hand and felt like he was handing over some of that strength to her. She indeed felt empowered, ready for the next step in her recovery. She left his office and entered the lobby. Colt ran into her on her way.

"Hey. What's going on?" Colt asked. He smiled.

"Oh, hey. I was just talking with Mr. Kingsley."

"You in trouble?"

"Oh, no. Just asking him for some help with some stuff I'm working on."

"Anything I can do?"

"Uh, no. But thanks." She felt the need to keep her search for a new place to live to herself.

Hannah walked into the break room and bought a soda. Her mind drifted towards one of the healthy relationships in her life—her brother, Michael. She trusted Michael, held respect for him, and felt a sense of loyalty from him that was not apparent in many relationships she had. Hannah felt a strong desire to talk to him about the next step in her journey—that of trying to get into an apartment.

During break, she made a phone call to Michael.

"Hello?" he answered.

"Hey, Michael."

"Hey, sis."

"Can you talk?"

"Sure."

"What are my options for moving into an apartment?"

"What does your doctor say?" asked Michael.

"She says if I moved home I should live in an apartment, to be more independent."

"Okay."

"So, I guess I'll go home and do some research and look at some."

"Sounds good. How are you going to get home?"

"Um. I'm not sure yet. Let me figure that out."

"Okay. When you do, let me know."

After she got off the phone with Michael, Colt entered the break room.

"Are you ready for some fried chicken tonight? It's Friday," he said.

"Mm hmm. Fried chicken night. How could I forget?" said Hannah.

"Hey, you want to walk outside with me during the rest of our break?"

"Sure."

They walked outside away from the camera monitors situated throughout the building. Then they chatted good-naturedly. For a moment, they paused from talking and just enjoyed standing together. Then Colt spoke.

"Wow. Relationships, huh?" He grinned at Hannah, referring to their recent topic in group therapy. They both laughed nervously.

"Have you been in many relationships?" he asked carefully.

Hannah paused a moment. "You mean, with other guys?"

"Well, yeah."

"I didn't know if you meant friendships with anybody or..."

"No, I meant how much have you dated?"

"Oh, okay. I dated off and on growing up. Had a high school boyfriend. I fell hard for a guy in college," said Hannah.

"How did it turn out?"

"Not so good."

"Oh, I'm sorry."

"It's okay. I learned, you know, from it," said Hannah.

"What happened, if you don't mind me asking?"

"No, I don't mind. I was very interested in loving God. He wasn't, although at first he pretended to be."

"So that must be real important to you? Uh, loving God?"

"Yes. God is a big part of my life."

They didn't speak for a few minutes. Then Colt spoke again.

"I would like for God to be a bigger part of my life."

"Really?"

"Yeah. I pray to Him sometimes. But I'd like to understand and know Him better, you know: how He thinks, what He wants."

"You seem to understand that He is a person."

"Oh, yeah. I have always thought of Him that way," said Colt.

"Me, too. I think of Him as a father," said Hannah.

"Huh, that's cool. I need a father."

"Yes, I remember you saying that your dad wasn't around much. Were you raised by your mom?" asked Hannah.

"Yeah. I don't know what it's like to really have a father. What about you?"

"Oh, my father was very involved in my life."

"Really?

"Yeah. He really took an interest in the sports that I played," said Hannah.

"That's important. I remember how you said he took you fishing and all. That's cool," said Colt.

Hannah and Colt didn't speak for a few minutes. They both were deep in thought.

"So, how do you love God, exactly? I mean what do you do? How do you love Him?" asked Colt.

"Well, to love God means you do what He says."

"Okay. Huh. What does he say to do?"

"The two greatest commands in the Bible are to 'Love the Lord your God with all your heart and with all your soul and with all your mind' and to 'Love your neighbor as yourself.' That comes from the book of Matthew, chapter twenty-two, verses thirty-seven and thirty-nine."

"So…I guess that means…that to love God is to love Him with everything you've got and to love other people?"

"Yes, that's right."

"But how do I love Him with everything I've got?"

"He will show you. Just read His words in the Bible so you can get to know Him better. And trust Him. Pray to Him. Ask the Holy Spirit to show you."

They were both silent for a few minutes. Then Colt spoke.

"Where do you get your positive attitude?" he asked.

Hannah thought a second. "I guess I just think that if I am positive about my situation, then I will notice when good things come my way. Someone told me that once," said Hannah.

"Huh. I never thought about it like that before."

"You should be positive about your life, Colt. I think you have a lot of things going for you."

"Like what?"

"You're smart, kind, and thoughtful."

"Thanks, Hannah."

After talking for about ten minutes, Hannah decided to take a risk and ask Colt a more personal question.

"So, how do you feel about how you got here?"

Colt fidgeted uneasily, looked at the sky, and let out a deep sigh. Hannah wished she could eat the words that just came out of her mouth.

"I'm sorry," she said. "I guess I'm getting too personal."

"No," he said. "It's okay. It's just that I'm going to see the judge this afternoon after group. He's the judge that diverted my sentence and sent me here to try to get better. I'm worried that he will send me to jail. It all depends on how he thinks I'm doing here."

"Do you think you have a good chance of staying in the program?" asked Hannah.

"I don't know. Mr. Kingsley is going with me to speak on my behalf. If he gives a good report, then I will probably get to stay here."

"I bet it turns out okay. Just be positive."

"Right. Be positive. Be positive like Hannah."

Hannah laughed.

They talked for a few more minutes and then went back inside to group. The day passed slowly. At the end of their session while they were waiting for the van, Hannah saw Colt and Mr. Kingsley get in a truck and drive off. She hoped for the best for him and longed for him to present himself well to the judge.

11

Colt's Story

A BEAD OF SWEAT rolled down the side of Colt's cheek as Mr. Kingsley gunned his truck onto the interstate. Colt wiped the sweat away and tried to control his breathing. Mr. Kingsley noticed.

"You okay, man?" Mr. Kingsley asked.

"Uh, yeah. Just a little nervous."

"Okay. Take slow, deep breaths to lower your heart rate."

Colt took a deep breath, filling up his lungs, and slowly released the air.

"You worried about the judge?" asked Mr. Kingsley.

"Yes, sir."

"I intend to give a good report about you. I can see that you are working hard. How's it going with your parents?"

"Not so good."

"What's going on?"

"My mom doesn't understand my illness. I think she thinks I'm weak because my mind isn't working right."

"Oh." Mr. Kingsley paused. "What about your dad?"

"He's not around."

They were quiet for some time.

"So, tell me about Matthew, the guy who is pressing charges against you," Mr. Kingsley said.

"Matthew and I got in a major fight over a girl about a week before we went hunting that day. The girl dumped both of us, but Matthew blamed me."

"So, when you went hunting the day of your incident, was Matthew upset with you?"

"I thought he was being cold to me, but he wasn't a jerk or anything. I just thought he was still mad at me."

"Did you shoot your rifle near him?"

"Yeah. Just as I fired my gun, he bent over to tie his boot right in front of me. I barely missed him. I promise I didn't mean to."

"I believe you. But you're going to have to make sure the judge believes you too, okay?"

"Yes, sir."

"How are your hallucinations?"

"I see people sometimes. Not a lot. Just at weird times, I'll see someone standing in the corner, and I think I'm the only one who sees them because they just fade away after a while."

"Be sure you tell the judge that, too. He needs to know that you need to be in our outpatient services and not in jail."

"Okay."

They rode the rest of the way in silence, both men apparently deep in their thoughts.

When they got to the courthouse, Mr. Kingsley instructed him: "Tuck in your shirt and straighten your collar. If you have a pocket knife, leave it here in the truck. You won't get past security with it."

Colt, a country boy who wouldn't go anywhere without his trusty pocket knife, reluctantly emptied his pocket and put the knife in the glove compartment. They entered the building, found the right courtroom, and sat on one of the pews in the viewing section, waiting for their turn to speak.

When Colt's name was called, he stood up straight and tall and approached the podium with Mr. Kingsley to address the judge. His roper boots made a significant thud with every step. The judge was a stern man who appeared to be in his sixties and didn't have time for empty conversation.

"Colt Freidmont has been very compliant with our treatment, your Honor," said Mr. Kingsley.

"Even though he has a debilitating illness, Colt goes out of his way to be nice to people. I see him interacting with our other clients in a positive way and showing up at group on time. He always respects me and shakes my hand when I see him. I think the program is good for Colt, but I also think that Colt is good for the program. I really would like to see him continue through the program and graduate."

After Mr. Kingsley finished speaking, the judge addressed Colt himself.

"Mr. Freidmont, you realize that you can never handle a gun again."

Colt swallowed hard. "Yes, your Honor."

"Is it true that you didn't aim your gun at this Mr. Matthew Senegal?"

"Yes, sir. I wasn't aiming at him."

"What were you aiming at?"

"I thought I saw a man standing about fifty yards away from me, aiming his gun at me, but I think I was hallucinating."

The judge paused. "Does this hallucinating happen often?"

"Actually, it doesn't happen a lot. Just sometimes."

"Do you feel like the program is helping you?"

"Yes, your Honor."

"How?"

"I'm learning how to take care of myself and respect people better."

"That's good, Mr. Freidmont."

After some more discourse, the judge made his final statement.

"Do you still have a plea of not guilty by reason of insanity?"

"Yes, your Honor."

"Okay. Well, seeing that you are doing well in Mr. Kingsley's program, I am keeping you on probation for two years. I need you to get through this outpatient program with flying colors, understand?"

"Yes, your Honor," Colt breathed deeply.

As they drove back in the truck, with the weight of concern lifted off his shoulders, Colt spoke candidly with Mr. Kingsley.

"I've been a redneck all my life, hunting with my buddies every chance I could get." He furrowed his eyebrows. "That kind of life is over for me now. I can never have a gun? I can't believe it. I can never have a gun. I started hunting when I was ten years old, and now I can never hunt again."

The last words out of his mouth hung in the air like thick smog.

"I love being out in the woods. I love the smell of pines. I love the excitement of the hunt."

"Yeah, you're going to have to find another hobby."

"I guess I could hunt with a slingshot."

"Now, that's an option."

The two men chuckled.

"You realize that not possessing a firearm not only protects other people but also protects yourself, right?"

"Yes, sir. It's just hard to get my mind wrapped around it. I also have a problem with not being able to drink with my friends."

"Is that due to the medicine you are taking?"

"Yeah. I can't have any alcohol mixing with the prescription drugs in my system." Colt swallowed hard again. Talking about these things was hard for him, but his feelings just seemed to pour out of him at the moment.

"Sounds to me like you need to reinvent yourself, Colt."

"Yeah." Colt's voice dropped with a tone of discouragement.

"What's on your mind?" asked Mr. Kingsley.

Colt paused for a moment. "I feel like I got a raw deal when I started having symptoms of my illness."

"What do you mean?"

"It just all seems so unfair."

"Kinda feeling sorry for yourself?"

"Yeah, I guess so."

"You know, in life, we all get our own hand to play from a deck of cards. Your hand may be different from someone else's, but you still have to play the hand you're dealt. There's just no getting around it. Some other guy may wish he's got your hand, and you may wish you had his. But it doesn't work that way. You have to work with what you got. Just play your hand, Colt, the best way you know how."

"Sounds tough," said Colt.

"You're headed in the right direction. Just be creative in what your new life will be after you get out of the program. You've just got to dream differently now. Start thinking about some new dreams you could have that include you dealing with your illness."

"Yeah, okay. Thanks, Mr. Kingsley."

Mr. Kingsley's truck reached the men's house where Colt was staying.

"Hang in there, man," said Mr. Kingsley.

They shook hands before Colt exited the truck.

"Thanks so much, Mr. Kingsley," said Colt.

As Mr. Kingsley drove off, Colt walked up to Sam and Sydney, who were seated in the garage finishing up the last drag of their cigarettes.

"Guess what?" asked Colt.

"What?" asked Sydney.

"I'm still on probation. No jail time, baby!"

"Cool," said Sam.

"I need to celebrate, too. The judge gave me probation," said Sydney.

"Whoo-hoo! Yeah!" yelled Colt, giving Sydney a high five. Colt sat down with the other two, and they chatted about the upcoming football game. Talking together, the three men showed a sense of camaraderie.

"So, Sydney, what's your story? What happened the other night that got you in lockup?" asked Colt.

"Oh, this fireman," said Sydney. "He was such a jerk. He was yelling at everybody to get out of the way while the other fireman took care of Mr. Paul. The first guy wasn't doing anything special. Just mouthing off at people. Then he brushed passed me real aggressive-like. I was so mad, so I hauled off and decked him. Felt like I needed to put him in his place. Then he called the police and pressed charges. We got into another scuffle after the police arrived, and they broke us apart."

"You have a short fuse, Sydney?" asked Colt.

"Oh, yeah. Gets me in trouble all the time. But you know what really causes me trouble?

"No. What?"

"Drugs. Been struggling with drugs since I was just a kid."

"Is that why you're here?" asked Colt.

"Yeah, I came here after rehab."

They paused for a moment in silence. Colt looked over at Sam, who seemed to be lost in thought.

"Sam's a deep thinker," said Colt, teasing the young man whom he barely knew.

Sam blinked, sat up, and leaned forward. "You know why I'm here?" asked Sam.

"Shoplifting? I see how you snatch cigarettes from people," said Colt.

"No, man, no. You see, I'm here because I'm an alcoholic, and I'm bipolar. That's a dual diagnosis. My mom said she could help me stop drinking by paying for my rehab. This is my third time in this outpatient program."

"Why is it your third?" asked Colt.

"I would do okay for a while and not drink. Then my ex-girlfriend gets in touch with me about something, and talking with her drives me crazy. Then I start to drink again," said Sam.

"Sounds like you need to dig deep to find a reason to stop drinking," said Colt. "Your ex-girlfriend gets to you, huh?"

"Yeah. She's merciless," said Sam.

"Keep her far away from you, bro," said Colt.

"Way far. As far as forever," said Sydney.

Sam turned toward Colt to ask him a question. He had mischief in his eyes.

"Why are you looking at me like that, man?" asked Colt.

"I was just wondering something about you," said Sam.

"What's that?"

"Since I'm talking about the ladies, I got to ask you. What's going on with you and Hannah?"

A shy grin came upon Colt's face.

"Ah, I knew it!" said Sam.

"What?" asked Colt.

"You like her, man. Oh, yeah. You like her a lot."

Colt conceded. "Yeah, I like her, but I'm just taking it slow. We've become friends, and that's all for now."

"Yeah, I know your type, man," said Sam. "The ultimate gentleman."

Colt nodded and smiled again shyly. He hid his eyes under his baseball cap and laughed. Sam and Sydney laughed and punched Colt in the arm.

As they were joking with each other, Ms. Rosie walked up.

"How did court go today, Colt?" she asked.

Colt straightened up and got serious. "Oh, it went well. I get to stay in outpatient."

"That's good to hear. You keeping your nose clean?"

"Oh, yes, ma'am. Absolutely."

"You know we do search checks when y'all leave to go to your centers. Ain't no drugs or paraphernalia going to be found in my house, right, gentlemen?"

"Yes, ma'am, yes, ma'am, that's right," the three men answered together.

"Got fried chicken tonight. Y'all hungry for some good food?"

"Yes, ma'am," the three men answered together again.

Ms. Rosie walked inside the men's house while the three men kept talking outside.

"Ms. Rosie means business. She's cool. But she means business, yes sir," said Sydney.

The other two men nodded in agreement.

EVENING CAME QUICKLY, and the residents of The Refuge inhaled Ms. Rosie's cooking. She called everyone to the men's house, so the women went over there to eat with the guys. Colt sat by Hannah, but they didn't talk. Nobody really talked at dinner, a somewhat unspoken rule in the group home.

After they ate, everyone settled in their rooms, as usual. Torrie came over to talk to Hannah, who was sitting on her bed watching TV.

"Hey," she said.

"Hey, Torrie."

"I really miss home. I really wish I could go home. I wrote a letter to my parents."

"How do they feel about you being in the group home?"

"My parents were the ones that actually contacted Ms. Rosie and sent me here after I got out of the main hospital," said Torrie.

"Oh. Did your parents respond to your letter?" asked Hannah.

"Not yet."

"What did you tell them?"

"I told them that I was feeling better. I miss home so bad." Torrie paused. "I miss home so bad it hurts right here in my stomach. It makes my gut ache inside."

"Yeah, that's rough."

"So how do you handle being lonely?" asked Torrie.

"I try to be positive. And pray. Pray real hard that God will bless your life and that you will be able to go home soon," said Hannah.

"Okay. I hope it works."

"I hope so, too. Have a good night."

"You, too. Thanks for listening."

"Sure," said Hannah.

Torrie left to go to her own room. Hannah turned off the TV and settled in for bed. She was grateful for the conversation with Torrie. Even though Hannah was usually quiet, she really needed people sometimes.

The house got very quiet. Hannah searched her thoughts and could think only of what Torrie said about being homesick. Everyone probably felt homesick. When they lay down on their beds at night, they each probably came to one thought. Everyone—Colt, Sydney, Sam, Torrie, Amanda, Sophia, Daphney, and Hannah—were probably thinking the same thing: When am I gonna get out of here and get on with my life? When can I live on my own? When can I go home?

12

Pop

HANNAH WAS HAVING cabin fever. She needed to be able to get out of the group home and do some things for herself. In a conversation with her parents, she found her answer to how she was going to get home to look at apartments.

"Hey, Mom," she answered to her mother's phone call.

"Hey, Sweetie. We are coming into Houston this weekend so your dad can see his Parkinson's doctor on Monday."

"Is everything all right?" asked Hannah.

"Yeah. It's just his regular check-up."

"Okay, then I have a suggestion," said Hannah.

"Okay. What is it?"

"I've been wanting to get home to look at apartments."

"How will you get back to Houston?"

"I could take my SUV back."

"Are you sure you're ready to have that kind of independence?"

"Yes, ma'am, I think so," replied Hannah.

"Okay. Just do what you need to do."

"Thanks, Mom."

Her father's health was failing. Making a four-hour trip one way would be taxing for him. He usually slept most of the way on these rides. His lack of stamina explained why he and Hannah's mother had not visited Hannah earlier. Hannah was in deep emotional turmoil over her dad's failing health. Her concern for him was intense, and sometimes she felt overwhelmed with sorrow at his decline.

The weekend came quickly, and Hannah's parents arrived soon to stop by and pick her up.

"Hey, Daddy," she said when they drove up to the group home.

"Hey there, kiddo."

"You're lookin' good, Pop."

"Thanks."

Moments existed now and then when her dad was thinking clearly and could communicate well. Other times, he was lost in his own world, trying to understand what was going on. Today just happened to be a good day, and Hannah was grateful.

Hannah loaded up her luggage in the trunk of the car and took a seat in the front passenger side of the car.

"Hey, babe," said her mom.

"Hey, Mom. Thanks for coming to get me."

Her mom was a strong woman. Over the years, she had endured the bouts that Hannah experienced with her illness. Hannah's recent visit to inpatient had been especially hard.

Outpatient was better than the main hospital, though, and Hannah remained grateful and positive about her whole progress in the outpatient program. Initially, Hannah had felt quite nervous and scared about going into the extended treatment program. The last program that she attended during her last hospital stay was in a different hospital, and she found outpatient services there to be horrible. The therapist who led Hannah's group back then was very mean and insensitive, and Hannah did not feel safe with some of the other clients in the therapy group.

While Hannah had been in inpatient treatment this time, she had spoken with Dr. Mitchell about her options.

"Dr. Mitchell, I'm not so sure I want to go into an outpatient program."

"Tell me why."

"Well, the last outpatient program I went to was not good at all."

"What do you mean?"

"Well, the therapist was really mean, really cold."

"I see. Well, I don't know any of the therapists in outpatient with this hospital that are unkind."

"I just don't know if I can take that chance."

"Why don't you let me get the director of outpatient, Kingsley, to come over and speak to you about their program."

"Okay," said Hannah.

"Do you think that would help?"

"Yes, ma'am."

"Okay, I'll set it up."

"Thanks."

The first time that Hannah had met Mr. Kingsley, he had come over to see her while she was in inpatient treatment. In contrast to his large football build was a deeply tender spirit. Hannah instantly liked him.

"So, Dr. Mitchell said you were having reservations about our outpatient program."

"Yes, sir. I had a bad experience in the last program I was in."

"Well, let me assure you, we treat each client with patience and sensitivity. I think you will like it there."

"In the last program I went to, the other clients were really hateful to me," said Hannah.

"We have a strict policy about harassment. I don't think you will have a problem with us. Was it really every client that gave you a hard time?"

"Well, a couple of the people there were nice to me."

"There. You see? Being a little positive is a good thing. I bet if you're positive about our program, you will see good things come your way. And I will personally keep an eye out for you. I'm trying to be positive about my life, too. It's hard to do, I know."

Hannah felt comforted by his response. "Okay, well if it's okay with Dr. Mitchell, then I would like to try your program."

"Good. I look forward to seeing you when you head over our way."

Hannah and Mr. Kingsley shook hands, and he gave her a big smile.

AS HANNAH RODE BACK with her parents to her hometown, she thought about that first visit with Mr. Kingsley and her present experience with the outpatient program. She felt very connected to a few of the other clients there. In fact, she even considered them friends. She felt closest to Colt, and she couldn't imagine not being able to talk with him.

Hannah's thoughts turned to how she had ended up here. Earlier in the year, she was a workaholic madwoman. She was working hard at her job, trying to be the best she could be. She started to lose sleep, and that issue became a big problem for her. Each night, processing her thoughts about her busy day consumed her, leaving little time to sleep. She was, above all, a thinker.

Holding a regular job had been very difficult for her. She still received government assistance to pay for her medical expenses, food, and shelter. She had to report her income to her caseworker when she was employed. When she realized how sick she felt, she decided to quit her job. Her resignation came too late though, because a week later, she was in the main psych hospital, struggling to think straight.

She didn't seize the illness in time to avoid tanking into mental confusion and fear. Her symptoms became full-blown, her brain imploded, and the voices came to attack her, worry her, and confuse her. Once the voices started to harass her, she struggled just to make it through the day. The excessive dialogue going on in her mind made handling the world outside almost impossible. Only an effective antipsychotic medicine could rescue her from the mental agony she struggled to endure.

"How's it going with the program?" her mom asked, interrupting Hannah's thoughts.

"It's going well. I'm learning a lot."

"What are you learning?"

"Coping skills, you know, how to deal with life."

"What kind of coping skills?" asked her mom.

"I meditate on peaceful things a lot. I read. I watch the news. I like to listen to relaxing music."

"I'm glad that's helping."

"So, how's Dad doing?" Hannah asked, referring to her father dozing in the backseat.

"He has good days and bad days."

"How is his thinking?"

"He gets confused sometimes. Sometimes he has a hard time concentrating, and he forgets what he's doing."

"Is that the Parkinson's?" Hannah asked.

"Yeah."

"That must be hard for him," said Hannah.

"Yeah. I think it is."

"That makes me sad."

"Me too."

Hannah could hear her father breathing peacefully in the back seat. She was grateful that he was resting. She thought about a time when she rested so peacefully when he had been in the driver's seat, when their roles were reversed. She remembered one of the first times he took her fishing in the bayous of south Louisiana.

In her memory, they woke up early, around four a.m. A fog settled on the ground, creating a misty heaviness. Her dad prepared some snacks, brought the tackle, and stashed a roll of toilet paper in a waterproof bucket that sat next to the gas tank in the boat. They were ready.

Half asleep, Hannah lay with her head next to her dad. An hour and a half passed before they reached the landing. Hannah woke up in a stupor. Her dad backed the trailer into the water, and Hannah got out and guided the boat with a rope tied to the front of it. She held the boat close to the dock.

With lifejackets on, they climbed into the boat. Her dad gunned the old, gasping motor, and they hit the bayou waterway in the swampland. Soon they were on their way, and her dad had a spot in mind where he thought Hannah could catch some fish. After about twenty minutes of riding through the main causeway, they reached a quiet place in the water and pulled in to anchor. A large stump from a cypress tree sat just below the water. Hannah worked quickly to squeeze a slimy worm onto her hook and cast it into the water, her cork bobbing close to the boat.

She felt a nibble on her line, and then the cork was quickly pulled under. She pulled back, set the hook, and reeled in a beautiful, small bream, just big enough to keep. Her dad took off the fish, tossed it into the igloo, and Hannah hurried to bait her hook again. No sooner was the worm in the water than an unlucky fish took the bait, and Hannah won another catch.

After thirty minutes, she had ten bream in the boat, and Pop was overjoyed at his daughter's success. He even caught some bass himself, on some fancy lure. They fished many years together, but no trip was as special as that first ride home with a boatload of perch. Those fish soon became fried food that had "slept in the Atchafalaya last night," as her dad would describe it.

BACK TO THE HERE AND NOW, Hannah knew this trip home from Houston was a good idea. She could hear her dad snoring in the back seat, and she was grateful that he was still with her. She knew he was slipping further into his illness, and she hurt for the day when she would no longer be able to greet him, tell him she loved him, or take off his ball cap and kiss him on his smooth, bald forehead. She truly loved him, and she was her daddy's little girl.

Hannah didn't know how many days her dad had left, and she desperately wanted to be with him, just to watch football or read the newspaper together. She had grieved deeply and cried frequently over the loss of his presence when she was in inpatient treatment. He was a dear, gentle, humble man, and she could not imagine life without him. Now she was able to see him, and she was very grateful.

They stopped at a burger restaurant for a break. Pop got a cinnamon roll. He was very efficient and neat in the way he ate. He used the napkin and plopped all excess into the paper bag that the food was served in without getting his hands sticky from the icing. He drank his beverage in utter contentment.

What a man he was. He knew when to work hard and when to rest. He knew what the weather would be like each day before it began. He knew when and where the hurricane was coming. He could recognize any kind of bird flying in the sky. He could enjoy himself simply watching a football game. In his younger years, he had been an avid reader. In his older years, he mentioned to Hannah that the only real important book to read was the Bible. Pop was a man with a backbone, a steady man who was faithful to his wife; and he was a good father, financially providing whatever his family needed.

RIDING HOME, HANNAH felt very safe. Her parents had been her faithful advocates for the many years that she had suffered with her illness. Now Hannah needed to return the favor by taking care of herself. She was determined to stay on top of her medication, to take good care of her hygiene, and to love herself as much as they had loved her.

Hannah remembered when her dad used to help her when she was fighting her illness at home. He would get her to take short showers by timing her to motivate her to take care of herself in an efficient manner.

"Okay," he'd say, standing outside the bathroom door. "You've got five minutes. I'll start the stopwatch when I hear the water running."

"Okay," Hannah would call out, determined to please him. Even though she didn't take short showers now, she was still thankful her father took such an interest in her.

He would also walk around the neighborhood with Hannah, sometimes bringing the dog with them. The memory of her walks with her dad was priceless. One time, when she was in one of her hospital stays, her dad had brought her dog on the visit, and both Hannah and the dog were overjoyed to see each other. Sometimes there was nothing better than the affection and admiration from a dog to cheer her up, and Pop knew that.

THE REST OF THE RIDE home from Houston was fairly quiet. Pop went back to sleep. Hannah was thinking logistically about how she was going to get back to the group home in her SUV. She asked her mom, who mentioned something that would help.

"I got you a GPS so you can find your way around the city with your SUV," said her mom. Hannah's phone and car did not have a built-in GPS.

"Oh, wow. Thanks, Mom," said Hannah.

"After your dad and I got lost coming over to see you, I realized that I didn't want that to happen to you."

"Yeah. That's going to be a big help."

Hannah was grateful for her mom who was looking out for her, even though she wanted and needed to be as independent as possible. Something she had sensed from going to the outpatient program was that she needed to be as stable as possible on her own. She wasn't sure how she was going to achieve that goal. She was so needy with her illness. She never imagined that things would ever be different than living with her parents indefinitely. However, she was beginning to think she could live by herself now, even with the burden of managing her illness. Maybe she could achieve the sense of autonomy that she was hoping for.

Hannah thought about her last talk with Mr. Kingsley at outpatient before heading home. She had left their conversation feeling a deep satisfaction about her situation in life. She was moving ahead in her recovery. She was feeling good about herself. Her confidence was growing. She felt a strong sense of security steadily growing inside her. Deep in the core of her being, she was starting to feel solid and whole. All she needed to do was keep going, one moment at a time, and trust in a God who loved her.

13

Dog Therapy

WHEN HANNAH AND her parents arrived at her parents' house, she was greeted by their precious dog, Penny. Hannah bent down and let Penny sniff her breath so she could discover what Hannah had eaten earlier that day. Then Hannah buried her face into Penny's fur, inhaling deeply. She loved the smell of dog dander.

Penny was a mutt, a mixture of who-knows-what, but she looked like some sort of terrier. She loved Hannah dearly, but Penny knew her true master was Hannah's dad. Pop loved dogs and took care of Penny, giving her heartworm medicine once a month, checking out the condition of her skin, and feeding her good dog food every day.

As a child growing up, Pop had a family dog who was his best friend. He took his dog, Josie, everywhere he went. She was some sort of terrier mix, too. She never left Pop's side. They often went hunting and fishing together in the woods. Pop knew the value of having a loyal, faithful dog as a companion. He had passed along his love for dogs to Hannah, who also saw the benefits of having a dog for a pet.

Since Pop was using a walker now, he couldn't take Penny on their evening strolls. Penny was also showing signs of her age. Her hips were stiff with arthritis, but she still liked to go exploring outside.

"Hey, Hannah, how'd you like to take that mutt on a walk?"

"Sure, Pop. Come on, Penny."

Penny recognized the word "walk," and she was immediately at the door, restlessly waiting for the door to open. She wagged her tail fiercely. Hannah put the leash on her, and off they went.

The February air was crisp and cold. Their breath left condensation in the air, and Hannah's lungs felt good in the cold. The walk was nice, and Penny enjoyed the time immensely, eagerly sniffing everything she could. She also saw two cats that she wanted to chase, but Hannah held the leash firm and wouldn't let Penny take off running after them. After the curious dog sniffed what seemed like every blade of grass, the two walked back to the house. Hannah felt relaxed and happy after the walk.

After Penny drank a good bit of water, Hannah coaxed the dog to her bed, a large pillow full of stuffing. Then Hannah petted Penny for a long time. She scratched her behind her ears and under her chin, and she petted her back and tummy. As they looked at each other, their eyes glowed with utter contentment. Hannah knew that when a person looks in a dog's eyes and sees contentment, their brains release a special chemical that makes both the human and the dog feel good. Petting a dog was great therapy for Hannah.

Penny wasn't the only dog that Hannah was crazy about. In the past, her close friend, Sharon, often asked Hannah to dog sit for their chocolate lab, Chloe. While home, Hannah paid a visit to Sharon and Chloe after she finished spending time with Penny. Chloe loved to fetch, and Hannah and Chloe were good friends. When Hannah came to the door, Chloe sensed right away that she was near and began barking excitedly. When Sharon opened the door, Chloe turned around and around in circles, eager to play. Hannah petted her, and all three went out in the backyard for a game of fetch. Hannah chunked the ball far out into the yard, and Chloe retrieved it. They played for some time. Both dog and friend enjoyed being together immensely. Finally, they went back inside so Hannah and Sharon could visit.

After talking with her friend and petting Chloe some more, Hannah got in the car and headed to the animal shelter outside of town. A very special dog named Scout needed a visit from an old friend. Hannah had known Scout, a rat terrier, for many years. Scout was a permanent resident of the animal shelter, due to her difficult temperament. Hannah and Scout were good friends. When she reached the room where Scout was living, Hannah walked in and talked gently to the dog. Scout wagged her tail and walked in a shy manner over to Hannah. Scout had weak interaction and poor socialization skills. Socializing dogs was the main service Hannah liked to volunteer for at the shelter.

Hannah picked up the dog, hooked a leash to her collar, spoke to her gently, and carried her outside. She put Scout down, and the terrier immediately began sniffing around, her nose to the ground. A hunter by nature, Scout loved following scents when she was outside. After they spent much time together, Hannah brought the dog back inside and played catch with her with a toy. Scout played very aggressively, probably trying to work out the stress she felt from living at the shelter. When they played together, Scout sometimes nipped at Hannah's hand, but Hannah knew that the dog was a difficult case, so she didn't take it too seriously.

Hannah tried to pet Scout, but the troubled dog would have none of it. Instead of taking to Hannah's gentle touch, Scout snapped at Hannah. The dog's eyes were wild and intense. Hannah wanted Scout to experience that chemical release in her brain just like Penny and Chloe did when Hannah petted them. Scout's eyes, however, showed pain and agitation. Hannah was very sad for the little dog. The anguish in Scout's eyes made her think of the similarities between people and dogs.

The state of the eyes of a creature, whether it was an animal or a person, told a story. She knew that Penny and Chloe had healthy eyes because they knew the security of a loving home, but Scout had unhealthy eyes. She was soul sick. Hannah couldn't help but think about the residents at her group home. She could see a lost look and an emptiness in the eyes of some of the clients there. Hannah reasoned that homelessness can affect animals and people in a similar way, preventing them from having real contentment in their lives. The eyes really could reveal what was going on inside—in both man and beast.

THAT EVENING AT her parents' house, Hannah watched her favorite movie, a film about a soldier living in Indian territory. She noticed in the film how the soldier made friends with a wolf and how he kept trying to feed the animal a piece of beef from his hand, but to no avail. Eventually, slowly, carefully, the wolf took the risk one day and strained forward to grab the meat from the soldier, signifying trust in their relationship. Just like that scared wolf, Hannah was gradually, carefully, trusting God more and more to provide for her in her growing independence. Watching the film was just another incident during Hannah's stay at her parents that revealed similarities between animals and people.

When she thought about the movie and how she needed to trust God more in her own life, Hannah realized that she could not live without her faith. She leaned on her relationship with God to give her a sense of fortitude. Mostly, she leaned on Him so much because she often felt so weak that she knew she couldn't live without Him. Without God, Hannah was nothing. She prayed, "Thank you, God, for my life. I'm so grateful."

God had played an important role in her life growing up. Hannah looked to God as her Heavenly Father. Her relationship with Pop helped considerably with how she viewed the Creator of the universe. God and Pop were a good bit alike. They were both loving and caring. They both had wisdom. They both provided encouragement. She needed that kind of attention if she was ever going to continue in independence.

Hannah was taking more and more steps towards that independence. The next night in her parents' home, Hannah went out to dinner with a good friend named Sarah. Sarah was a petite woman with cute clothes and a straight, pixie haircut.

"So, how's it going?" asked Sarah.

"Things are going pretty well—I just wish I knew where I was going to live after the group home. That's the hard part—wondering and waiting," said Hannah, feeling conflicted inside.

"How can I help you?"

"I need to look at apartments here to see if I can afford it."

"I can help out with that."

"Really?"

"Sure, I will check out some places this week while you are in Houston."

"Wow. I really appreciate that," said Hannah.

"What are you looking for?"

"A cheap, one-bedroom apartment in a safe area."

"Okay. How cheap?" asked Sarah.

"If they have rental assistance, that would be nice."

"Okay. I will look into it."

"Thanks so much, Sarah. How are you doing?"

"Fine. The boys are doing well."

"Good. Ready to eat?" asked Hannah.

"Definitely."

THE WEEKEND WENT by quickly, and Hannah started getting homesick even before she left her parents' house. By the time she geared up to go back to the group home, she was not ready to leave. On Sunday morning, she went to church with her parents before she hit the interstate. She realized how close she was to many people there, as she was greeted and hugged during and after the church service.

The sermon was very appropriate to her life at the time. The pastor spoke on "Facing Life's Storms." She was in a storm in her life right now. The winds of uncertainty and insecurity were blowing fiercely. She needed an anchor. She knew that anchor was her hope in God.

Her pastor spoke about believing the promises of God, and he said that every person needed at least ten promises from God to get through the storms in their lives. She knew some from the Bible. She focused on a number of specific scriptures, and these Bible verses, along with the medicine in her body, helped to keep her mind focused. The medicine really helped, balancing out all those erratic neurotransmitters. Perpetual sanity was in her reach.

After church, with her clothes already packed in the trunk, Hannah ate lunch with her parents before hitting the road. They headed to a special restaurant to get a good home-cooked meal.

"So, what's your goal for this week, kiddo?" asked Pop, who was munching on a piece of tasty pot roast.

Hannah thought for a moment. "I want to stay positive about my situation and live in the moment."

"Sounds good," he smiled.

She said goodbye to her parents and teared up as she pulled out of the restaurant parking lot. Inside her heart, she felt a tug of longing to stay at home with them to keep tabs on Pop. Her mom was taking good care of him, but Hannah still just simply wanted to be with him. She felt the immediate angst of separating from him.

Driving by herself in her SUV was a huge advancement in her recovery. She still faced a long journey in feeling self-confident, but driving in the big city was a huge accomplishment.

"I can do all things through Him who strengthens me." She repeated in her mind the Bible verse from Philippians, chapter four, verse thirteen, for a few moments. She put on some upbeat music; and after a while, the tears dried, and she was singing down the highway. Driving her SUV was going to open up bigger opportunities for her as she continued through the outpatient program. Cruising down the road and singing, she looked up at the sky and felt hope for the future, especially the immediate future.

HANNAH ARRIVED AT the group home around three in the afternoon. As she pulled into the driveway, she was immediately met by Ms. Rosie, who was sorting used clothes in the garage.

As Hannah was getting out of her SUV, Ms. Rosie spoke firmly.

"I need to talk to you about your driving in town."

"Okay," Hannah replied, somewhat nervously. She was afraid a bomb was about to hit.

"I need to know why your doctor ordered for you to be able to drive every day."

"Because driving on my own helps me become more independent," said Hannah.

"But do you have appointments every day?"

"No ma'am, but I do different things every day. One day I might go to the coffee shop. The next day I might go to get a burger. The next day I might go to the dog park. It will change every day."

"Okay," said Ms. Rosie reluctantly. "But I need you to let me know where you are from time to time. Just text me so I won't worry."

"Okay. No problem," said Hannah.

Ms. Rosie's firm, motherly voice changed to a light-hearted tone.

"We've got fried fish tonight."

"Great."

Hannah breathed a sigh of relief after their conversation. She hated conflict. She understood, though, that Ms. Rosie was responsible for her and needed to know where she was, especially in a big city.

Hannah grabbed her luggage and headed into the house. She felt the familiar heat as she trudged upstairs and plopped her stuff on her bed. She sat down on her comforter and sighed, feeling tense from driving in Houston traffic.

Torrie walked by Hannah's door and knocked on it.

Hannah looked up.

"Hey, Torrie."

"Hey. How was the trip?"

"Oh, it was good."

"That's good."

Torrie paused a moment. "Uh, I was wondering if I could move into your room."

Hannah thought for a few seconds. "Did you ask Ms. Rosie?"

"Yeah, is that okay with you?"

"Sure. Did she say it was okay?"

"Yeah, I actually told her I would like to room with you," said Torrie.

"Really?"

"Yeah, you seem like a nice person."

"Well, thanks, so do you."

"It's hard to find nice people around here," said Torrie.

"Why do you say that?"

"Well, I used to room with Carla, and she really made my life miserable."

"How?" asked Hannah.

"She took my clothes when I wasn't looking. She also had a creepy smile on her face that made me feel weird."

"Oh, I've noticed that about her, too."

"Really?"

"Yeah, she was standing over my bed one time when I woke up," said Hannah.

"Gosh. Creepy."

"Yeah, I know. Carla is hard to understand. Sometimes she is outright aggressive. Other times she's kind of passive-aggressive with that creepy smile," said Hannah.

"She's a very selfish person. I don't like selfish people," said Torrie.

"Me neither."

Hannah began hanging up her clothes that she had brought back from her trip.

"Mind if I turn on the TV before I start moving in?" Torrie asked.

"No. Go ahead."

Torrie turned the TV immediately to The Brady Bunch.

"Oh, The Brady Bunch. I love The Brady Bunch," said Hannah.

"Oh, I do too. Simpler times, huh?" said Torrie.

"Yeah. Very simple. Sometimes I wish I could live my life the way they did. No complications. No worries. A good life," said Hannah.

"Yeah. To have a life like that would be good. I miss my old life. I still can't believe I'm here sometimes." Torrie changed the subject. "I made a strawberry cake today. Do you want a piece?"

"Sure."

The two women walked down the squeaky stairs into the kitchen and helped themselves to the dessert. They sat down at the kitchen table to eat. Hannah noticed that Torrie was speaking in a more animated tone, and she was making sense. *Her meds must be working,* Hannah thought.

"How long were you in the main hospital before you got here?" asked Hannah.

"Two weeks."

"How did you find out about The Refuge?" asked Hannah.

"My caseworker in the main hospital told my parents about it."

"That's how I got here, too."

"Ms. Rosie really helped me out by letting me stay here."

"Yeah, I had nowhere else to go either," said Hannah.

They talked for some time. They were both the same age and had grown up in the same generation, so they reminisced together about different topics. The two women chatted away and began to feel even more comfortable in each other's company. They found a connection—a bond that is unusual to find under such circumstances.

Hannah was grateful for her new roommate. She also was grateful for her outpatient program and some of the people she met there. She was grateful for Ms. Rosie. She was thankful for all the good people in her life. She knew that good, close, supportive relationships were key to her recovery. Her grateful heart led to her endurance during her whole stay at The Refuge.

14

Resiliency

AT FIRST, HANNAH COULD hardly believe that she was so much more self-sufficient. On Monday morning, Hannah got into her SUV and drove on the interstate to the outpatient program the same way they rode in their van. She felt so fulfilled that she was taking this next step in her progress. More independence was in her sights.

She was reunited in her outpatient group with Colt, Sydney, Sam, Martha, and Andrea. She felt more comfortable with her group, and she was ready for a good day. She filled out her twenty-four-hour sheet and noted that her coping skills were watching TV, reading, and meditating.

Each person was in their own little world. Martha and Sydney were coloring. Colt was playing with his phone. Andrea was sleeping. Sam was sprawled out on the floor with his face up to the radio, talking to it. Hannah started to draw a design on her coffee cup when Ms. Jordan walked into the room.

"Good morning, guys," she said.

"Good morning," said the group, each person still focused on what they were doing.

"Sam, I need you to take a seat," said Ms. Jordan.

"Okay," said Sam reluctantly, leaving the voices from the radio and getting up to find a place on one of the couches.

"Today we are going to talk about emotional resiliency," said Ms. Jordan. "Does anyone know what resiliency means?"

A pause emanated in the room.

Then Hannah spoke. "It means that you have strength," she said.

"Good, Hannah. Does anyone else have a definition?"

"It means that you're tough," said Colt.

"Good, Colt. Today, I am going to tell you six aspects of emotional resiliency. The first one is this." Ms. Jordan turned to write on the board.

"Emotional resiliency is realizing what is in your control and what is not in your control. You are only responsible for owning your own behavior. What do you think that means?"

Sydney spoke. "That means if someone does something bad, it's not your fault, it's their fault."

"Good, Sydney," said Ms. Jordan. "That's right. You have to take care of yourself, and sometimes that means letting another person crash and burn in their own choices so that they will learn from them. That brings us to our next point in emotional resiliency, which is this: Develop good self-care habits. What do you think I mean by this?"

"That means you take care of your hygiene," said Sam.

"Yes, Sam, that's right, but it also means that you take care of your emotions. What can help us take care of our emotions?" asked Ms. Jordan.

"Journaling," said Hannah. "Writing down how you feel about something to get it out and on paper."

"Yes. Journaling is a good way to take care of our emotions," said Ms. Jordan. "Talking about them with someone you trust is another way you can take care of yourself. Now, I want everyone to give me one word to describe how they feel. Let's go around the room."

"Tired," said Andrea with a big yawn.

"Concerned," said Colt, lifting his eyes to the ceiling.

"Strong," said Sydney. He took a deep breath and exhaled.

"Worried," said Sam, as he fiddled with his thumbs.

"Insecure," said Martha. "I feel very insecure."

Then Hannah spoke. "Grateful," she said.

"Okay. Good," said Ms. Jordan. "Let's talk about another way to be emotionally resilient. How about developing compassion? How can that make us strong?"

Martha raised her hand. "Caring about someone besides you means you aren't selfish," she said.

"That's right. Good," said Ms. Jordan. "You can also be emotionally resilient if you use events as learning experiences and be flexible when new events come your way."

Hannah was furiously writing down everything Ms. Jordan was saying. She found the discussion extremely helpful. She looked around the room and noticed that everyone was leaning forward and really listening to Ms. Jordan. Even Andrea was attentive in the midst of her sleepiness. They were all engaged.

"Another point I want to make is that you need to limit the hostility factor," said Ms. Jordan.

"What does that mean?" asked Sam.

"That means that you restrain from aggression when reacting to an event. Don't blow up or react strongly when something upsetting happens to you. Let the event soak in and then evaluate how you feel about it before you respond."

"That's hard to do, Ms. Jordan," said Sydney.

"I know, Sydney, and that brings me to my final point about emotional resiliency. You need to strive for goodness and not perfection. Sydney, if you get mad about something, be mad: just don't hurt anyone with your anger. Be good. But remember, you don't have to be perfect. You are human."

After Ms. Jordan finished speaking, she gave a piece of paper to everyone to journal their emotions. They all took their time with this assignment.

In her journal, Hannah wrote, "I feel like I'm making progress in the program, but I still feel unsure about a lot of things. I want to be a better person, but sometimes I think I'm too hard on myself. I don't know where to draw the line between pushing myself and letting myself just be me. That's a delicate thing to consider. I know I'm still a perfectionist. I don't know how hard to push myself. I pushed myself too hard last year and that's how I ended up here. I realize now that I need to be very gentle with myself when I deal with stress. I need to love myself when I start placing expectations on my performance level when tackling a job. I need to be okay just being Hannah. I need to be okay with accepting myself for who I am and not push myself so hard to be ultra-productive. I have been so hard on myself for so long, I think it's time to ease up on Hannah. I need to love myself for who I am, taking the good and bad in stride. I don't have to accept my bad habits, but I can allow myself to be imperfect, to be allowed to fail, to be allowed to be human."

When Hannah finished journaling, she breathed a deep sigh. She looked up and noticed that everyone else was finished and staring at her. Obviously, breakfast was next on the agenda. Hannah smiled weakly. Ms. Jordan spoke.

"Okay, time for breakfast. Good session, you guys."

At breakfast, Hannah sat with Colt, and they talked about what they had learned that day.

"So, are you emotionally resilient?" she asked Colt.

"I don't know. I don't think I reacted well when I shot at that man—I mean, when I shot at the hallucination that I thought was a man."

"But you were trying to protect yourself, right?"

"Yeah."

"And you were trying to protect the guys with you?"

"Yeah, I really was."

"Did you know it was a hallucination at the time?"

"No. I really thought it was real."

"I don't think you should beat yourself up about this. You made a mistake, but you're a good person, Colt."

"I don't ever want to make that mistake again."

"I know, I know," said Hannah.

Colt looked at Hannah and, in an unusual moment, his eyes misted over. "Thanks, Hannah," he said genuinely.

"You're welcome," said Hannah, looking into Colt's eyes and recognizing that she had touched a part of him that was very real. She realized that Colt thought he was a bad person for what he had done. He didn't accept that he was just trying to take care of himself and his friends when he shot at the image of a man. Hannah thought her words helped him come to terms with that fact. In their conversation, Hannah was helping Colt take care of his emotions about why he entered the outpatient program. She was glad that she could be a friend to him.

As Hannah rode back to The Refuge in her SUV that afternoon, Hannah thought about what they talked about that day. She thought deeply to let the information soak in. She felt like she needed to be emotionally strong as she steadily got better.

AS THE DAY BECAME evening, all the women at The Refuge were doing their own thing, waiting for supper. Hannah was seated in the den, watching football. Suddenly, Amanda burst through the front door and shouted garbled, unrecognizable words. Then she bounded up the stairs, still shouting. She apparently was intoxicated.

Mr. Paul was back in the house after his episode in the men's home. He never really had a stroke—the experience was apparently just an occurrence of high blood pressure which was now controlled with medication. At present, Mr. Paul was in the kitchen when he heard Amanda carrying on upstairs. He headed up the stairs after her. She shouted at him to leave her alone. The next moment, Hannah saw Mr. Paul holding Amanda from behind with his arms locked around her stomach. Even with Amanda as big as she was, Mr. Paul was still able to drag her downstairs. Amanda had a distant, confused, drunk look on her face. Mr. Paul dragged her outside and plopped her on the sidewalk in front of the house. Then he came back inside and locked the door.

Wow, Hannah thought. *Amanda just got kicked out.*

Immediately there was fierce knocking on the door. Mr. Paul came out of the kitchen and opened the door.

"Can I come back in?" asked Amanda.

"No. Sober up," said Mr. Paul frankly, and he shut the door in her face.

Hannah wanted to let Amanda in, but she didn't dare cross Mr. Paul, whom she respected. Besides, if she wanted to be emotionally resilient like they talked about in group, then she needed to stay out of other people's business and let Amanda be responsible for herself.

About an hour later, Amanda knocked again, this time more softly and soberly. Ms. Rosie was there, and she let her in. She proceeded to initiate a serious sit-down talk with Amanda in the dining room. Since Hannah was in the next room, she heard the whole conversation.

"Do you understand why I am upset with you?" asked Ms. Rosie.

Amanda gave no response.

"I know you are aware that there is to be no drinking in this house. If you drink outside the house, you can only come back if you are sober."

Again, no response.

"We've been through this before. You know you cannot handle alcohol. Don't even go there. I care about you, but I cannot help you if you continue to drink."

"I know, Ms. Rosie. I know."

"If this happens again, I will be forced to send you back to rehab, and I know that you don't want that."

"Yes, ma'am."

"So, are we on the same page? We understand each other?"

"Yes, ma'am."

"Okay. Go upstairs and get cleaned up."

"Yes, ma'am."

A very humbled Amanda walked upstairs to take her shower. She made a mistake, and she was owning her own behavior.

As Amanda was walking up the stairs, Daphney came down and walked into the den. She started up a conversation with Hannah, who had not really talked to Daphney personally since Hannah's first day there. Hannah did not know what to expect.

For a moment, they were both quiet.

"So, you like having your car here?" Daphney asked.

"Oh, yeah, I like to drive," answered Hannah. She felt like a more pointed question was coming next.

"Do you think you could take a trip with me?"

Hannah looked into the dining room and saw that Ms. Rosie had left.

"Uh, what do you mean?" asked Hannah nervously.

"I want to go to Florida to see my family. Do you think you could drive me?"

Hannah paused, not knowing what to say.

"Oh, no. I'm sorry. Ms. Rosie won't let anyone ride with me in my car. It's a pretty strict rule."

A pause of silence filled the air. "Okay. Just thought I'd ask, you know."

Daphney got up quickly and left the den, and Hannah took a deep breath, letting the air out slowly. Staying out of people's drama was harder than she had anticipated. She really wanted to be a friend to Daphney, but Hannah needed to set her boundaries.

Late that night, while she was in bed, Hannah heard a commotion outside her door. Sophia and Daphney were talking in hushed tones, but Hannah could make out what they were saying after she quietly cracked her door open.

"How long will you be gone?" Hannah heard Sophia ask Daphney.

"I don't know. I'm not sure," said Daphney.

"Call me when you get there, okay?" said Sophia.

"Okay. I'll be okay. Don't worry," said Daphney.

Hannah heard Daphney walking downstairs. She heard the front door open and shut. Daphney slipped out into the night and was gone. Hannah eased slowly out into the hallway as quietly as she could so she would not wake up Torrie.

"Hey, Sophia," whispered Hannah.

Sophia was sitting on her bed. "Yeah?"

"Where's Daphney going?"

"She's going to catch a bus to Florida to see her family."

"Oh, okay. Does she have any money?"

"I think so. I think she saved some up."

"I guess she was just real unhappy here," said Hannah.

"Yeah. I think so."

"Are you happy here, Sophia?"

"I don't know. Not really."

"How come?"

"Well, I don't really have a family to go home to."

"Oh."

"I can't just take off and go home like Daphney."

"Yeah. My doctor doesn't want me to live at home because she wants me to get an apartment so I will be more independent," said Hannah.

"So, you can't go home either."

"No, I can't."

They were silent for a few moments, weighing the gravity of their conversation and situation in life.

After talking with Sophia, Hannah decided to go to bed.

"Okay. Well, night," she said.

"Night," said Sophia.

Thoughts raced through Hannah's mind as she got back in bed. She felt like she should do something for both Daphney and Sophia. How would Daphney get to the bus stop at this time of night? How would she pay for the bus ticket? Should Hannah go out and find her?

Then she thought about Sophia. How could she help her find an apartment? She seemed so young to be on her own.

After about thirty minutes of chasing thoughts in her mind, she decided to be sensible. Daphney was a grown woman. She could probably take care of herself. Sophia was growing up. Maybe the group home would be good for her for a while. Still, Hannah was caught between wanting to help more and wanting to protect herself. She concluded that she was at The Refuge to get better. She was there to learn to be emotionally resilient. She wasn't there to be everyone's rescuer.

Hannah realized that there was a fine line between helping someone and enabling them. In the past, she had been an enabler in relationships and didn't want to be one now to the people around her. She knew that everyone was responsible for their own thoughts and actions, just like she just learned in outpatient that day. She was learning that truth now more than ever since she came to the group home. She wanted to be emotionally resilient. She wanted to be strong. She decided to stay put and got back in bed.

Before Hannah nodded off to sleep, she told herself that she needed to take care of her own needs and let others take care of theirs. That personal decision would make all the difference in her going back to her hometown someday. With that thought, she drifted off to sleep, and another day at The Refuge was laid to rest.

15

Anxiety

HANNAH WAS SO CONCERNED with all the drama that was going on at The Refuge that she decided to check out another group home. She wanted to see what another place was like. When she got to outpatient that day, she woke up Andrea, the sleeper, and asked her about how she liked her group home.

"It's okay," said Andrea, sitting up to talk to Hannah.

"Who is your group homeowner?" asked Hannah.

"Her name is Ms. Libby."

"Do you have her number?"

"Yes." Andrea gave the number to Hannah and slouched back down on the sofa, dozing off again. At break time, Hannah called this Ms. Libby and asked if she could come over for a visit.

"Is there something wrong at your group home?" asked Ms. Libby to Hannah.

Hannah replied, "I just wanted to check out my options."

"Okay. Come by this afternoon."

Hannah could hardly wait until group time was over.

Ms. Jordan opened group with the familiar question: "Okay, is there anything special that you guys would like to talk about today?"

The group was silent for a moment, thinking to themselves.

Then Hannah spoke. "Can we talk about how to handle anxiety?" Not only was Hannah anxious about visiting the new group home that day, but she also felt an inner unrest about her future living arrangements.

"Sure," said Ms. Jordan. She wrote the word "anxiety" on the board. She continued. "Why do you guys think we have anxiety? What causes anxiety?"

"Worry. Worry causes anxiety," said Martha, smacking her lips.

"Okay, good." Ms. Jordan wrote "worry" on the board. "Anybody else have a reason for anxiety?"

"If something bad is going to happen, it makes you anxious," said Sam, his knee bobbing up and down.

"Good, Sam. Anybody else?"

"When I don't live in the present, I worry about the future, and those thoughts makes me anxious," said Hannah.

"Okay," said Ms. Jordan. "Now what can we do to relieve anxiety?"

"I take a pill for anxiety," said Martha.

"Yes, medication can help. Anybody else?"

The group was silent.

"I'm just going to list some things that you can do to help with anxiety." Ms. Jordan wrote on the board. "Your coping skills will come into play here a lot."

She listed ten ways to help with anxiety: eating healthy, taking supplements or special medication, resting, meditating, listening to soothing music, exercising—like walking, doing yardwork or other work outside—deep breathing, talking out your problems with someone like a counselor, engaging in pet therapy, and practicing positive self-talk.

"Have you guys ever practiced breathing techniques?" Ms. Jordan asked.

"I did in the inpatient hospital," said Hannah. "In our therapy group, we would breathe in, then hold it, then exhale."

"Yes, that's very good. We are going to do that right now. Everyone sit up straight in your chairs and hold your shoulders back. Andrea, I need you to wake up. This is important."

Andrea sat up slowly, reluctantly, appearing groggy. The others sat up straight, waiting for Ms. Jordan's next command.

"Now, we are going to breathe in to a count of four."

Colt, Sam, Sydney, Martha, Andrea, and Hannah all took deep breaths.

"Okay, now hold that breath to a count of four." They all obeyed. "Okay, now release and exhale to a count of four."

The six clients exhaled slowly, feeling the oneness of them all breathing together. Hannah felt relaxed.

"Good. I want you guys to practice this every day and see if it helps your anxiety. Now, it's break time for breakfast. Y'all go relax and take it easy for a while."

The group stood in line for breakfast, ate quickly, then scattered.

Hannah followed Colt outside.

"Hey," said Hannah.

"Hey," said Colt. "That was cool that you brought up the topic of anxiety. Good call."

"Thanks. I think I've had anxiety all my life. I can remember having a lot of butterflies before my soccer games. And that lasted for ten years. That's a lot of anxiety."

"Yeah, I used to get nervous before football games. I think some of that is part of the deal."

"Yeah, anticipation and getting your body ready to compete is normal. It's just that I also get anxious when nothing is about to happen," said Hannah.

"Why are you anxious now?"

"I feel nervous because I don't know where I will end up in the future. I am thinking of moving back to my hometown, but I am also thinking of staying and living here in Houston."

"It's hard to deal with anxiety," said Colt.

"I know. Sometimes prayer helps me."

"That's cool." He paused and then changed the subject. "After you leave outpatient, are you going to work?"

"No, I am on disability."

"Oh," said Colt.

"Yeah, I have a lot of friends at home that I could visit with if I moved," said Hannah.

Colt looked into Hannah's eyes. "I will miss you if you move," he said.

Hannah looked back at Colt, seeing the sincerity on his face, and she felt touched.

"I will miss you, too," she said gently.

They stood out in the cool air and said nothing, just content to be together. She wanted to take his warm hand and hold it in hers, but she decided against it.

After she got out of outpatient, Hannah used her GPS to find the address to Ms. Libby's group home. She texted Ms. Rosie that she was going for coffee, which was true, but Hannah decided to stop by Ms. Libby's on the way to the coffeehouse.

What she discovered surprised her. The door to the house was wide open, and she entered the dark environment carefully. In the dim light, she saw several guys sitting on a sectional couch, watching TV. The den was dank and undecorated. The energy in the room felt very heavy.

Ms. Libby wasn't there. Hannah spoke with the house supervisor to ask if she could have a look around. He agreed, and she walked into the women's bedroom to check out the scene. A woman sat on one bed, with another bed next to her unoccupied. There was no carpeting on the floor and no special décor in the room. Quite frankly, the place just didn't feel like a home.

On the ride back to The Refuge, Hannah compared Ms. Libby's house to Ms. Rosie's home. Ms. Libby had given little attention to making the environment warm and inviting in her group home. Ms. Rosie's house, on the other hand, was full of accents and pictures and matching furniture. Every room had its own special theme with inspirational frames on the walls. Every Monday was a day for cleaning, and Ms. Rosie cleaned the house from top to bottom, all the way down to wiping off the bed frames.

There was simply no comparison. Ms. Rosie's house won out by a landslide. On the issue of surroundings, Hannah was in a good place, and she knew it. As for the pervasive conflict in the home, she would deal with it as it came. The conflict was part of the atmosphere of a group home, probably all group homes. She was not leaving.

When Hannah arrived back home at The Refuge, she immediately went to the laundry room to check and see if any of her clothes were dried and ready for her to take back to her room. She had noticed that some of her clothes were missing, so she was determined not to lose any more. She suspected that maybe Amanda had taken them since she was a large woman like Hannah and probably wore the same-sized clothes.

Amanda wasn't home yet, so Hannah decided to do some investigating. She walked up the staircase and into Amanda's and Daphney's room. She walked into the bathroom where the closets were. The bathroom door was broken and open, so she had to work fast before anybody came in. She felt uneasy and sneaky, but if Amanda took her clothes, they would be in Amanda's closet, so she thought she might as well nose around. She began rummaging through the closet and, not to her surprise, found a couple of shirts and a pair of jeans that were hers.

Hannah was determined to check the laundry room every day right after outpatient to make sure she got first dibs on checking her clothes. She also decided that she would periodically check Amanda's closet for any stolen articles. She decided not to confront Amanda about taking her clothes since Hannah was somewhat afraid of Amanda, to begin with.

Just as Hannah shut the door to the closet, she turned to find Amanda standing in the doorway to the bathroom, looking straight at her. Hannah immediately and instinctively gasped.

"Uh, hey," said Hannah nervously, quickly jerking the clothes behind her back.

Amanda said nothing. She was preoccupied and headed for the toilet. Apparently, she hadn't seen Hannah going through her closet. Hannah breathed a sigh of relief and went back to her room to put up her clothes. Her heart was pounding. She sat on her bed and took deep breaths like they had in group that day. Inhale deep, hold it, exhale slowly. Inhale deep, hold it, exhale slowly.

BEFORE DINNER, HANNAH WAS in her room with Torrie. They were watching The Brady Bunch and relaxing, enjoying each other's company. Suddenly there was a commotion downstairs. Hannah's ears perked up, and she heard Daphney's voice. She was back.

"Torrie, Daphney's back. I can hear her downstairs," said Hannah.

"Really? Wow. I'm going to check things out and find out the scoop."

"Okay, yeah, go investigate."

Torrie went downstairs for a few minutes and came back up again.

"Daphney went to Florida to see her family, and they sent her back here on the bus. She really stinks, too. I think she peed herself."

"What happened?"

"I don't know. I didn't get any more information, yet."

They heard a very vocal discussion about finances between Ms. Rosie and Daphney downstairs. They were having an argument because Daphney used most of her disability check for that month on her trip to Florida. Plus, Ms. Rosie wanted Daphney to take a shower and get cleaned up. Above all, hygiene was a virtue to Ms. Rosie. Daphney headed upstairs, shouting to be left alone.

"Daphney, take a shower!" yelled Ms. Rosie.

"I ain't got to take no shower!" Daphney yelled back.

"Daphney, take a shower! I'll bring you your clothes!"

"I ain't dirty! I don't need to take a bath!"

Ms. Rosie came upstairs after Daphney. She spoke in a loud, firm tone to the rebellious client.

"If you don't take your shower, I'm shipping you off someplace else."

There was no answer from Daphney.

"I mean it, Daphney, get in the shower *now*."

Hannah and Torrie could hear Daphney stomp into the bathroom in the hall and slam the door. Apparently, she was staying because they could hear the shower water running.

"Wow, never a dull moment, huh?" asked Hannah to Torrie.

"She must have had a bad visit with her family."

"Yeah, that's too bad," said Hannah.

SOME TIME PASSED, and the clock showed that dinner was approaching. A freshly bathed Daphney came downstairs to eat. When she got to the table, she sat down in the seat where Amanda usually sat. Amanda came downstairs, saw Daphney, and put up a fuss.

"Hey! That's my seat," demanded Amanda.

Daphney looked up at Amanda and looked away, stating, "Not no more it's not."

"But that's where I always sit."

"Well, you ain't sitting here now."

"I always sit in that seat. You need to move."

Daphney stewed for a moment.

"Oh, all right. Man, Amanda, you need to relax."

Daphney got up and moved to a different chair.

"Satisfied?" she said, being antagonistic.

Amanda didn't respond but sat in her chair as if she had never left, and she smiled a small, pompous grin.

No one dared to ask Daphney about what happened in Florida with her family. Some things are better left unsaid. Later, after dinner, Daphney came into the den where Hannah was sitting and watching TV.

"My Florida trip didn't work out," confided Daphney.

"I'm sorry," said Hannah. "Did you see your family?"

"Yeah, I saw them, but they didn't want to see me."

"How come?"

"They think I'm a burden to them because of my mental illness."

"But you seem to be doing well," said Hannah.

"I know, but they don't see it that way."

"I'm sorry things didn't work out."

"Thanks."

Hannah was grateful to talk to her. Daphney and Hannah shared a moment of heavy, thoughtful silence. They watched TV for some time together. Hannah realized that she was very privileged to have her own parents in her life. She knew that family support was very important when dealing with a serious mental illness. She couldn't imagine life without her family behind her. *How hard it must be*, she thought, *to go through this alone*. Looking over at Daphney and seeing the sadness in her face made Hannah feel sad. Daphney had the lost eyes of a shelter dog.

AT FIRST, WHEN HANNAH was in college, no one understood Hannah's illness—not her friends, her parents, nor even herself. Hannah floundered in and out of college for a number of years before they found a doctor who could treat her. By that time, Hannah's parents were securely behind her, supporting her all the way. At the time, Hannah didn't realize how important that support was to have. Now, even though her parents couldn't be with her to support her in person, Hannah still knew that they were behind her. Since her brother was visiting her every weekend, she felt secure that she was not alone.

Just then, in the middle of her thoughts, Hannah got a text from Sarah in Louisiana, the friend who was looking for an apartment for her in her hometown. Hannah went upstairs to give her a call.

"Hey, Sarah," Hannah said on the phone. "What's up?"

"I checked out apartments for you. I looked at about five of them in safe areas. All of them are $600 to $700 a month for a one-bedroom. What's your budget?"

"Oh, that's way too expensive. That's almost all of my disability check."

"Okay. I haven't found any yet that have rental assistance, but I will keep looking."

"Okay. Thanks, Sarah. You doing okay?"

"Yeah. I'm okay. How are you feeling?"

"I'm homesick. But I feel strong," said Hannah.

"You do?"

"Yeah."

"That's good," said Sarah.

"Yeah. I want to be more independent. I'm a bit frustrated with my living situation," said Hannah.

"What's going on?"

"Oh, I just feel like my bed is all I have in the world, and even that's being rented."

"Oh, yeah. You have a car, don't you?" asked Sarah.

"Yes, I do. That's right."

Hannah realized that even in her limited situation, she was still richer than many people in other countries.

"I will keep looking for rental assistance," said Sarah.

"Okay. That's great. Thanks," said Hannah.

"No problem. I gotta go. I'm cooking supper."

"Okay. Talk to you soon."

"Bye."

Hannah hung up. She decided that the next day she would do some investigating for herself in Houston to see if she could find anything cheaper than $600 a month. How could she possibly pay for that with her disability check? She knew that the law required her to pay for her food and rent with her own money. How would she make ends meet? How would she live on her own? Maintaining her independence hung on securing accommodations. She was determined to find a place to live and not to worry so much about the future.

As she learned in class that day, she needed to use a coping skill to keep her from working herself into an anxious ball of knots. She concentrated on deep breathing and began to meditate as she often did when she was in her inpatient hospital stay. She focused in her mind on beautiful nature scenes and kept breathing deeply. She also tried to have positive self-talk. As she meditated, she said to herself, "I am bold, I am calm, I am courageous. I am bold, I am calm, I am courageous." Then, she listened to calming music on her MP3 player. After about thirty minutes, she went to sleep with resolve in her heart and confidence in her spirit.

16

Schizoaffective Disorder

IN GROUP THERAPY, Ms. Jordan was talking about some of the diagnoses that most of the group members experienced: major depression, bipolar disorder, schizoaffective disorder, and schizophrenia. She opened the class with a very thought-provoking question.

"Does anyone have any questions about their diagnosis?"

The group was silent for a moment. Then Colt raised his hand. "What are delusions and hallucinations?"

"Good question, Colt," said Ms. Jordan. "A delusion is a strong, irrational belief that cannot be swayed by a rational, realistic argument. A hallucination can be audio, like hearing voices, or visual, like seeing something no one else can see. A person who is hallucinating may also be able to smell something that no one else can smell or feel like they are being touched in a certain way when no one is really touching them. Delusions and hallucinations are symptoms of a psychosis."

"Why do I have them?" asked Colt.

"It's part of the symptoms of your illness. Do you want to tell the group your diagnosis?"

"Yes. I'm schizoaffective."

"Do you know what that means?"

"I think so. It is basically bipolar plus schizophrenia."

"Thank you, Colt."

Ms. Jordan stopped talking for a moment and let the quietness fill the room. Then she asked, "Does anyone want to talk about how they got here?

The group was still quiet. No one seemed to want to talk about their illness until Colt raised his hand again. He was being the brave one.

"Yes, Colt?"

"I would like to talk about how I got here."

"Okay. Go ahead. Nothing leaves this room."

Colt began slowly, methodically, carefully.

"I can't believe everything that has happened to me since right before I got sent to the main hospital. At the time, I was having these real drastic mood swings. One day, I was out hunting with some friends. We went out every weekend during hunting season. While I was looking for a buck to shoot, I started to feel weird. The sunlight seemed brighter than usual. The wind felt louder and creepy.

"Out of the corner of my eye, I saw a man about fifty yards away. He was set low in a crouching position. I thought he was just another hunter waiting for a good shot, like me. Then I noticed that he turned his shotgun towards me. Everything felt weird—really weird. I felt a sense of panic and lifted my shotgun without warning anybody. I heard a voice in my head that said, *Shoot him, he's going to kill you,* so I shot at him. Then he seemed to disappear into nothing, like he was never there, to begin with. 'What are you doing?' yelled Matthew, a guy who was with us. 'You almost shot me!' he yelled again."

Colt continued, "You see, he bent down in front of me to tie his boot right when I shot my gun, so it went off right above his head. He was really mad at me. When we got back to our trucks, he called the police on me. Then they took me to jail. A few months later, I came to the hospital as an inpatient."

"How do you feel right now, Colt?" Ms. Jordan asked.

"I feel real unsteady. All the lights in the room seem real bright to me. I can't believe it. I'll never be the same again. How will I ever have a normal life again? I will never get to hunt with my buddies. I will never be able to hold a full-time job. What's going to happen to me?"

"Have you told your doctor about your symptoms?"

"Yes, ma'am. He's trying different meds on me."

"Colt," said Ms. Jordan, "Have you told your doctor everything that you said today about how you feel about your illness?"

"No, I haven't."

"You need to let your doctor know everything that you are feeling, okay?"

"Yes, ma'am," said Colt.

"Okay, thank you for sharing, Colt. Does anyone else want to talk about their illness?"

Hannah raised her hand.

"Yes, Hannah, go ahead."

Hannah began to talk, and the words seemed to rush out of her like a river flowing over a waterfall. "I understand how Colt feels. My illness is schizoaffective disorder, too. When the disease is full blown and I'm having an episode of psychosis, it robs me of my life. An episode robs me of my personality, my real feelings, my ability to cope and function."

"How does the psychosis come over you, Hannah?" asked Ms. Jordan.

"Well, it depends. Sometimes, I go through a bout of mania for several months, then I fall into a depression, then I just slip into a psychosis. Other times, I might be under a great deal of stress for half a year, become manic, and then slip into a psychosis, or have a breakdown, as I often refer to it," said Hannah.

Hannah continued. "I'm going to miss out on a lot of things in life due to this illness. It just doesn't seem fair. I try to be positive and grateful for my life. I know that God has a plan for me in all this, but sometimes I just get so discouraged that I have this illness and that I can't do anything about it."

"Thank you for your honesty, Hannah," said Ms. Jordan. "There's something I want you to remember about your illness, and this bit of information goes for all of you. Your mental illness is both a part of you and not a part of you. It's you, but it's not you. Try to think of your illness like the saliva in your mouth. When your saliva is in your mouth, it's a part of you. When you spit, the saliva is on the ground, and it's no longer a part of you. That's the way I want you to think about your illness. It's a part of you, but it's not a part of you, at the same time. It's you, but it's not you. Maybe that will help you understand it better."

Ms. Jordan's explanation seemed to rest in each patient's mind, and a time of silence filled the room as each person appeared to reflect on their thoughts.

"Okay. We are hearing some good, honest things today. Who else would like to talk about their diagnosis?"

Ms. Jordan looked around the room and waited. "No one? Okay. Good group time. It's time for breakfast, everybody."

The six members of the group filed out and stood in line for their little boxes of cereal and milk cartons. Colt and Hannah sat together for breakfast. Then they went outside to talk.

"I don't like to talk about my diagnosis. There's such a social stigma about mental illness, even today," said Hannah.

"I know. I will talk about my issues in group because people here are cool. But out there, in the real world, I would never talk about my illness. No way. People so often associate fear with mental illness. It's not fair, but it's the way it is," said Colt.

"You know what I hate the most about my illness?"

"What?" asked Colt.

"The humiliation—the humiliation of being con- sidered part of the dregs of society, the humiliation of being out of control of your thoughts when you're in an episode, the humiliation of feeling the social stigma and the bigotry against people who have a mental illness," said Hannah.

"I know," said Colt. "I know how you feel."

"And you know what else I hate?" said Hannah. "Being misunderstood. I think some people expect more of me than I can give or do in my life. I'm always taking my illness into consideration when I decide to do anything—like join a group or volunteer or whatever."

"Yeah, and you know what I really hate?" asked Colt.

"What?"

"I hate all the slang terms used to describe people with a mental illness," he said.

"Like 'psycho,' you mean?" asked Hannah.

"Yeah, and 'freak,' 'wacko,' 'looney,' 'schitzo,'—I hate them all. One day, those words will be associated with prejudice and discrimination. One day, just wait, you'll see—it will be culturally wrong to say those words out loud," said Colt firmly.

"I hope so," said Hannah. "I hope you're right. When people hear the word, "schizo," in the word "schizo-affective," they freak out, I think," said Hannah.

They were silent for some time. Deep inside, Hannah wished they were in another time in the world, a time when prejudice against people with mental illnesses was nonexistent.

Then Colt broke the silence. "You know what, Hannah?"

Hannah turned to him.

"I think you are too strict with yourself about your illness," he said.

"Really, how?" Hannah asked.

"I think there are a lot of things you could do. You are very high-functioning."

"Really? That's nice of you to say." She paused. "I want you to know that I understand what you are going through, since we share the same illness. The delusions and hearing voices are brutal."

"Yeah, I know. They are," said Colt.

"I hate them," said Hannah. "I wish so bad I could turn back the clock so that I never would have lost my mind. I wish that I'll never lose my mind again," said Hannah.

Hannah's comment was a heavy thought. Her statement hung in the air like humidity on a hot day.

As they were standing there, talking, Colt and Hannah shared a moment of deep and mutual understanding. Such a level of insight shared had escaped Hannah in any previous relationship. She couldn't imagine feeling closer to someone in her whole life. Their diagnoses had joined them together. She felt that such friendships were rare. She was very grateful for Colt. She looked over at him, and her eyes met his. They both smiled at each other softly, understanding each other. They had reached a higher level of friendship, and Hannah felt deeply satisfied with her relationship with Colt. She told herself not to forget this moment and promised herself to meditate in the future on the immediate good feelings she was experiencing.

17

Forgiveness

A SURPRISE CAME FOR Colt and Hannah at the end of their break. For the second session of the day, a different therapist was in the room. She would become an important contact in Hannah's life. She was substituting for Ms. Jordan, who had left for the day. The new therapist's name was Ms. Carrie, and she had an interesting topic to discuss.

"Today, we are going to talk about forgiveness. There are four points I want to make to help you forgive the people in your life who have wounded you," said Ms. Carrie.

Hannah sat up in her chair and leaned forward. This topic was something she needed to hear.

"First," Ms. Carrie continued, "I want you to think of the people who have hurt you as sick and not bad people. If you think they are sick, then maybe you can forgive them more easily than if you just think a bad person has harmed you, and you want to get even with them."

Hannah thought about that point. *Huh*, she thought to herself. What Ms. Carrie just said was something that could help her. The people in her life who wronged her in the past maybe were not bad people at all. Maybe they were sick people—soul-sick people. Whatever was sick in their soul had led them to hurt Hannah. Their harmful actions were not intentional. In fact, she thought that maybe some of them were trying to act with good intentions, and they were confused about how to really help her. Thus, they failed out of ignorance and misdirection, guided by a sick soul. Hannah could forgive someone like that. She herself knew she had a sick soul, at times.

When Hannah thought about the soul sick people in her life, she thought most recently about her inpatient stay in the main hospital. She felt like many people there were intent on harassing her. Hannah had determined in her heart that she was not in the hospital to make friends and that she did not want to talk to anybody. She simply did not engage. She thought she probably had seemed cold and distant. One person verbally attacked her one time in group therapy. In front of everyone in the group, he personally attacked her self-esteem and self-worth. Hannah had turned the other cheek, but the therapist didn't do anything to defend her. She didn't say anything.

Hannah felt like the guy who had verbally attacked her was probably soul-sick, so she could forgive him. The therapist, on the other hand, was supposedly well, psychologically. Hannah struggled to forgive her.

"Next," said Ms. Carrie, "I want to point out that whatever you have been through has molded you into the wonderful person you are today. The hurtful experience you went through at the hands of someone else has made you a stronger person who has learned the benefit of perseverance. Don't reject those 'bad' experiences as something horrible. Embrace them as a situation that can make you better. Whoever did you harm, God can turn the consequences of their actions into something good."

Hannah never thought about this knowledge before. Maybe she could forgive the therapist who didn't defend her that day in group therapy. Her experiences in her past, both good and bad, helped to shape her into who she was right now. When she was not in the main hospital, she really tried to be a good friend. She wanted to do everything with her best effort. Could it be possible that the experiences of being deeply hurt by other people had led to the development of the good qualities that she had today? She found that idea remarkable.

Ms. Carrie proceeded with her third point on forgiveness. "The only behavior you can control is your own. You can't control the behavior of anyone else. If someone has behaved badly towards you, you can keep your distance from them, but you can't make them say they are sorry for hurting you. You can only change your own behavior, so stop wishing for reconciliation if you know the other person is hardhearted. All you can do is your part, which is to forgive."

Hannah thought about that point for a moment. What she wanted most from some people in her past was reconciliation, but she honestly didn't think that would happen. She could only change her own thinking, forgive them, and let the hope of reconciliation die. That thought was a difficult concept to digest.

Ms. Carrie made her final point. "If you feel so angry with someone that you want to take revenge against them because you think that getting even will make you feel better, then you are shackled to your offender. If you forgive, you free yourself from them and from any debt that you think they owe you. All you can do is leave revenge to your higher power and let the offender go."

Hannah knew that Ms. Carrie was spiritual because she talked about a higher power. Hannah decided to talk to the therapist when group was over to see if she did any personal counseling. For months now, Hannah had wanted a personal therapist. She most longed for one when she was an inpatient. At that time, Hannah met a few times with the group therapist privately, but having a few meetings was not the same as having her own therapist like Hannah was used to back home. She needed to vent and talk some things out, but the opportunity never arose. Maybe now was her chance.

When Ms. Carrie finished her talk, and people were leaving the room to go to lunch, Hannah approached her.

"Ms. Carrie, can I speak with you for a minute?" Hannah asked.

Ms. Carrie looked up from her paperwork and into Hannah's eyes. She showed a warmth and depth that Hannah didn't notice in very many people.

"Sure, how can I help you?" she responded.

"Do you do any private counseling?"

"Yes, would you like my business card?"

"Yes, ma'am, that would be great."

"Let's sit down here a minute to process some things."

"Okay." Hannah sat down in a chair at a desk, seated opposite Ms. Carrie. Everyone else went to lunch.

"What is your diagnosis?"

"I'm schizoaffective."

"How are you doing?"

"I'm doing pretty good. But I would like to look at old wounds and see how I could recover from them."

"Are these wounds from other people?"

"Yes."

"Can you forgive them?"

"Yes, but how do I deal with the hurt I feel every time I think about them?" asked Hannah.

"Well, we will always have bad or negative feelings tied to a hurt or a wound. That can be a good thing. Those feelings help us to avoid getting hurt the next time."

"Oh, okay."

"Just feel the feeling when it comes, and then let it pass."

"Can I ask you another question about forgiveness?"

"Sure."

"What about the forgiveness of God? What about the thought that forgiveness can occur in us when we recognize that we have been forgiven by God for our failures and mistakes, for all of our sins?"

"Well, Hannah, that's another good point about forgiveness. I didn't talk about that particular kind of forgiveness because I'm not supposed to bring religion into my lectures at the hospital."

"Oh, okay. Um. . . can I call you to meet with you sometime to talk about other things?"

"Sure. Anytime."

"Thanks."

Hannah left the room and felt good about their conversation. For some time, she had wanted to see a counselor who liked to talk about faith and spiritual matters, but she had never found one that she connected with the way she did with Ms. Carrie.

When outpatient was over, Hannah got into her SUV and made her way to the dog park, a place she located one time when she was on her way to get a burger. She loved dogs so much and just went to the dog park to be near them. Interacting with dogs helped her psychologically the way playing with Penny, Chloe, and Scout helped her in her hometown. She texted Ms. Rosie and let her know where she was going.

On the way to the dog park, an apartment complex just off the interstate caught her eye. The place looked like an average complex but not too posh. She saw many apartments that she knew she couldn't afford, but this one looked affordable. Hannah pulled off the interstate to check it out. She pulled into the parking lot of the complex and walked to the manager's office. The woman was pleasant and efficient.

"What do your apartments run for a one-bedroom?"

"$450 a month with a $450 deposit," said the woman.

Hannah was encouraged by this information. Maybe she could live in Houston. She weighed in her mind whether she should live in Houston or move back to her hometown. If she found an apartment here, maybe that was the answer she needed. She decided to call her brother, Michael, and discuss the matter with him. He had a level head and gave sound advice.

Back at the group home, Hannah called him that evening when he would be driving home from work. He answered on the first ring.

"Hey, bro," said Hannah.

"Hey, sis," said Michael.

"I think I may have found an apartment."

"Really? How much?" he asked.

"$450 a month."

"That's not bad. Let me talk to Mom about it."

"Okay. That would be great," said Hannah.

After she hung up, Hannah felt tremendous hope. Could it really be possible that she was going to have a place of her own soon? Her dreams of being independent seemed to be a close reality.

Feeling good about how things were going, Hannah picked up her phone and called Ms. Carrie, the therapist.

"Ms. Carrie?"

"Yes, this is she."

"This is Hannah from the outpatient hospital."

"Yes, sure. Hi, Hannah."

"I wanted to set up an appointment to meet with you."

"Okay, how about tomorrow evening around 7:00 p.m.? My office building is just off the interstate in north Houston. I will text you the address."

"That would be great."

"Okay, see you then."

Back at The Refuge, Hannah asked Ms. Rosie if she could go out for a late appointment the next night, and Ms. Rosie agreed. Hannah was so excited she could hardly contain herself from getting on her bed and jumping up and down.

THE NEXT DAY, all through outpatient classes, Hannah could think of nothing else other than seeing Ms. Carrie. She tried to think ahead of time what questions she might ask her. She felt prepared when she finally reached Ms. Carrie's office at ten minutes before 7:00 p.m.

"Hi," said Hannah.

"Hi, come on in," said Ms. Carrie.

"I know what I want to talk about," said Hannah.

"Okay, good. Let's get started."

Hannah took a seat. "I want to talk some more about forgiveness. There's some people I need to forgive from when I started having problems with my illness when I was in my early twenties."

"Okay."

After they talked for some time, Ms. Carrie suggested that Hannah do some journaling. "You need to pinpoint exactly what you are forgiving. Also, write out what the wound cost you and what were the losses in the relationship. You need to grieve those pieces in your heart that you are holding on to."

Hannah thanked Ms. Carrie after they finished talking. She drove home to The Refuge that night and thought deeply about the wounds she had received as a young adult. She entered the house and sat quietly on her bed, her journal in her lap. She opened the book and wrote down her thoughts.

"I realize that some people in my life who were trying to help me when my illness first hit were sincere, but they missed the mark. They saw me manic in the middle of a serious illness and didn't know what to do."

Hannah continued to write into the night. She went through each friend who had tried to help her in her first bout with her illness—the ones who really cared about her but struggled in their attempts to help her. Hannah thought about that time so many years ago, and she realized that she just wanted people whom she knew as friends to listen, to hear her, and to restrain from giving her advice. She just needed someone to hold her hand. Hannah went to sleep holding her journal close to her heart. She felt relieved about forgiving each person. She was glad she finally had something down on paper about these relationships and wounds.

When Hannah woke up in the morning, she was almost amazed at how she was feeling. She felt a strength in the core of her being that she had never felt before. She felt capable and resourceful. She was identifying her needs and making movement to get those needs met. When she thought about her outpatient program, she felt confident when she was around her peers who struggled with mental illness the same way she did. They weren't like her friends who first dealt with her illness out of ignorance so many years ago. For the first time in her life with her illness, she could identify with people who shared her same struggle, the struggle to stay sane. She finally felt understood at a level of understanding that general society couldn't give her.

As she got ready for the day, Hannah thought about how she felt about her therapy group. She had found people just like her, and she realized that she was not alone. For the first time in a long time, she felt genuinely happy. She felt happy because she had hope, genuine hope—the hope for sanity and the hope for a future of independence.

18

Bad News

THE NEWS HIT HANNAH in the pit of her gut as if someone just punched her in the stomach. Sitting in the lounge at outpatient while she was on break, Hannah received a text from her mom. "It doesn't look like getting an apartment is a possibility. I'm sorry."

Hannah felt dumbfounded by the comment. Why? What could possibly be the reason, if she could afford it? She decided to text her brother. He must have talked with her mom about how Hannah found an apartment in Houston. She texted, "Mom said I won't be getting an apartment. I'm so disappointed." She didn't know what else to write.

Her brother immediately called her and began to explain. "Yeah, I'm sorry you got the news. It doesn't look good for an apartment. If you got sick again and broke the lease, it would be a lot of money to pay for your debts."

"But what if I'm okay? How can you determine if I will break the lease?"

"I'm sorry, babe. It's just too risky right now."

They couldn't talk long because her brother was on lunch break. When they hung up, Hannah felt deeply disappointed. The euphoria left from the day before, and she fell into despair. If she needed to be on her own, like her doctor advised, then where could she go if not to an apartment? That meant she would have to stay in the group home indefinitely. How long would she have to live in the group home to prove she was healthy enough to be on her own? She was so discouraged, and she realized she was stuck—caught in a pit of sluggish mud that she could not walk through. She just laid her head down on the table in the outpatient lounge where she sat and closed her eyes. Tears began to escape out of the corners of her eyes. She was discouraged because after all that had happened with her since she came to Houston, she once again felt without hope, the way she had felt when she was in the main hospital. Sorrow swept over her like an overwhelming crash of waves coming in from the ocean.

Surely, she was not at the end of her rope, but she began to think otherwise. Some of the women at The Refuge had lived there for several years. She had been staying in the group home for four months. How could she possibly live there for years? She was so upset that she just picked up her lunch and threw it away. She normally loved food, but she didn't even feel like eating.

WHEN SHE GOT HOME from group that evening, her phone rang as soon as she climbed upstairs and sat on her bed. Her mom was calling her. Hannah answered immediately. As if she wasn't already dealing with enough, another bomb dropped.

Her mom spoke seriously. "Sweetie, your dad's not doing well. He fell earlier today, and we took him to the hospital."

"Oh, okay." Hannah felt her heart sink.

"Are you coming home this weekend?" her mother asked.

"I was planning on it."

"Good. Then you will be able to see him."

"Okay. I will talk to you soon."

When Hannah hung up, she said a quick prayer for her father—that he would not suffer terribly. She knew that his Parkinson's was progressing. This fall may have been a result of his illness.

Two blows hit her that day. No apartment was in sight, and Pop was in the hospital. The next day was Friday, and she would be leaving outpatient early to go back to her hometown to see her father. She was feeling very depressed and went to sleep tired.

The next morning, she got up slowly and unwillingly pushed herself to go to the program.

"What's wrong, Hannah?" asked Torrie, apparently noticing that Hannah was unusually quiet that morning.

"My dad's not doing well," said Hannah.

"Oh, I'm sorry."

"And I also found out I can't have an apartment."

"Wow. Bad news."

"Yeah."

When Hannah got into her SUV, her eyes welled up with tears. She drove methodically through misty eyes. She trudged into the outpatient building without hope. Colt greeted her at the door and immediately noticed something was wrong.

"Hey, Hannah. What's up?"

Hannah didn't feel like explaining herself.

"Having a bad morning," she said.

"Anything I can do?"

Hannah looked up into Colt's eyes and felt weary.

"Colt, will you...pray for me?"

She didn't know how deeply Colt connected with his faith, but she didn't know what else to say. She didn't know what else to do.

"Sure," said Colt, with a look of concern on his face.

Hannah dragged herself into the group room and slumped into a chair. She didn't care what was on the agenda to be learned that day. She didn't care about anything except her dad.

When asked by Ms. Jordan, Hannah said she was a one on the happiness scale. She might as well have said she was a zero. Her illness was being manifested in a severe mood swing. A few days ago she was happy, and today she was despondent. What an emotional rollercoaster to be on.

As Hannah sat in class, she pulled out her journal and began to write, "I don't know what to do. I am stuck in a situation, and I can't move forward. I have come to a place of uncertainty. I need to know that God is with me. I can't do this alone without Him. I know that God says, 'Never will I leave you; never will I forsake you' from Hebrews thirteen, verse five. I'm so grateful for that. I don't know what to do about my apartment. I just know I could live in one right now. How do I prove my health? I don't think I'm totally healthy, but I think that getting better will take some more time and growth inside of me. I think I can do that growing while I live in an apartment. I also don't know what to do about my dad. How will I live without him? I know he's fading. I wish I could live in my hometown and just spend all my time with him. And finally, I don't know what to do about Colt. How can I leave him and move back home? Every time I'm with him, I feel like we get a little bit closer in our friendship. What would I do without him?"

When Hannah finished journaling, she lifted her eyes and saw Mr. Kingsley standing in the doorway. Mr. Kingsley asked Ms. Jordan to see Hannah. She got up and followed him to his office, feeling unsettled.

"So, how are you doing, Hannah?"

"I'm not doing too good. My dad is sick. I'm going home today to see him."

"Well, I hope he gets to feeling better."

"Thanks," said Hannah, feeling no emotion. She was shutting down emotionally to try to handle the weight of what she was going through. She was in crisis mode, and she was trying to conserve all of her resources—her energy, her emotional strength, her determined will—so she could handle the storms ahead.

"Well, I will just get right to the point," said Mr. Kingsley. "I understand that you have been spending some time with Colt Freidmont."

"Yes, sir," Hannah looked at him, immediately feeling nervous in her stomach.

"Do you two have a serious relationship?"

"What do you mean?" Hannah thought that she and Colt had a very serious relationship, even if it was just a friendship.

"Well, I mean, are you two dating?"

"No, sir. Not exactly."

"What does that mean?"

"Well, we are not romantically involved, if that's what you mean."

"What does he mean to you?"

"He is just a very close friend. I feel like I understand myself better and why I'm here after spending time talking to him."

"Okay, I'm listening."

"Well, it's just that I think he makes my life better. I couldn't imagine not being friends with him here in out-patient."

"You know about our rule about personal relationships in the program, right?"

"Yes, sir." Hannah hesitated. "But if you don't mind me saying, I think making friendships here is one of the most important things I can do for my recovery."

"How so?" asked Mr. Kingsley.

"I just mean that when I connect with someone here on a deeper level because we share some of the same symptoms in our illnesses, the friendship makes me feel like I'm not alone. It gives me hope."

"Oh, I see." He paused for a moment. "But nothing romantic going on, right?"

"No, sir."

"Okay, I believe you. I will allow your friendship with Colt to continue. Just keep it as it is—a friendship."

"Yes, sir. I understand."

"Good. You can go back to group now."

Hannah got up, feeling relieved, shook Mr. Kingsley's hand in a spirit of understanding, and walked back to group. As she was walking, she breathed a deep sigh of relief. With everything going on in her life, she would have been devastated if Mr. Kingsley told her that she couldn't be friends with Colt anymore.

Since it was break time, Hannah went looking for Colt outside. He was getting some fresh air.

"Hey, Colt."

"Hey, how's it going? What did Mr. Kingsley want?"

"He asked about our relationship," said Hannah frankly.

Colt paused for a moment, then spoke. "What did you say?" Colt asked curiously.

"I told him we were close friends."

"Good, that's the truth, but. . .," his words trailed off.

"What?" asked Hannah.

"I was just thinking today how I'd like us to be more than friends."

Hannah paused. What bad timing. *He drops this on me right after Mr. Kingsley tells me no romance,* Hannah thought.

"I think being more than friends might be a possibility, Colt."

"Really?"

"Yes, but only after we get out of here," Hannah said firmly.

"Oh, you mean out of outpatient?"

"Yeah. You know the rules. Plus, I think we need some time out of here to get to know each other better. You know, we need to really go on dates and spend more time together," said Hannah.

Colt paused. "Yeah, I guess I understand." He sounded disappointed. He dropped his head and exhaled deeply.

Hannah was discouraged, too, but tried not to show her true feelings. She had given Mr. Kingsley her word. Besides, becoming romantic with Colt while they were still in treatment would be confusing. She would never know if the relationship was just an outpatient romance, or if it really had depth—even though she felt strongly that it did.

"Ready for group?" she asked him.

"Uh, sure, yeah," he nodded, and they walked inside.

At group time, Ms. Jordan asked everyone to describe themselves in one word. Colt started the answers.

"Concerned," he said, rubbing on a rock in his hand.

"Unwanted," said Andrea, coloring in a coloring book.

"Confused," said Sam, closing his eyes.

"Thoughtful," said Sydney, concentrating on the board.

"Hopeful," said Martha, smacking her lips.

"Unsure," said Hannah, staring into space.

"Okay, good," said Ms. Jordan. Whatever the therapist said after that escaped Hannah's mind. She started coloring and tuned everything else out. She was trying to cope with the difficulty that she was facing about where she was going to live and what was going to happen to her father. She felt so burdened she could hardly color, but doing artwork was a good coping skill, so she persisted in what she was doing.

Hannah stopped coloring for a moment and looked around the room. She thought about the people around her. She softly prayed for all of them. She prayed that Andrea wouldn't be so painfully shy. She prayed that Martha would participate more in class. She asked for God's guidance for Sydney that he would grow more and more into a strong man. She prayed for Sam that he would stop talking to the radio. She prayed for Colt that he would know in his heart what a special man he was.

Just after she finished praying for her group, Hannah asked Ms. Jordan if she could leave for the day since she was going home. Ms. Jordan agreed, and Hannah quickly gathered her things, softly said goodbye to Colt, and hit the highway. She put on some uplifting music and tried to focus on positive things. Everything had been going so well up until the last few days. She was progressing in outpatient and developing friendships in her outpatient group and in her group home at The Refuge. She just knew the next step was going out on her own. She felt that waiting in the group home would be excruciating. How would she survive?

Hannah tried to remember her coping skills that she had learned in group. Some of them came to her mind—meditation, breathing exercises, listening to music, reading, journaling, and talking with friends. She also realized that she needed to practice mindfulness—or living in the present.

Here is where the rubber met the road. Could she really use the skills she had learned and apply them right now? Would her faith hold for the duration of her stay at the group home? She focused on how beautiful the day was, listened to her music, prayed, and repeated positive statements in her mind. After four hours of deliberate concentration on the present and focusing on the music she was listening to, she found herself in her hometown, making her way to the hospital to see her dad.

When she walked into the hospital room, she noticed that her dad was disoriented.

"Hey, Pop," she said.

He immediately looked at her and said, "Hey, Hannah."

Hannah was relieved that he spoke to her. She wondered how badly he was really feeling. She motioned to her mom, who was seated next to her father's bed, to come out in the hall.

"How's he doing?" asked Hannah.

"He's not doing good. They won't let him out of the bed because they are afraid he's going to fall. This is really hard on him."

"Okay. What can I do?"

"Just sit with him and try to cheer him up."

"Okay."

They walked back into the hospital room. Hannah sat down next to her father's bed and talked to him. He didn't respond to her comments, and his brow was furrowed. She looked at her father's gentle hands. She took one of his hands and squeezed it hard. He squeezed her hand back, and they both smiled. Every positive moment meant so much to her.

When Hannah was driving from the hospital to her parents' house to spend the night, she thought about her dad and how much she had grieved for him when she was in inpatient treatment at the main hospital. She had often cried because he was failing at the time, and she didn't know if she would ever see him again on this earth. She was grateful now that she could spend some time with him.

When she arrived at the house, she decided to write him a poem to cheer him up. Hannah pulled her journal out of her book bag, grabbed a pen, and sat down at the kitchen table to write a few simple rhymes.

> When I think of you, Pop,
> How can I begin?
> You are my daddy,
> My very best friend.
>
> When I think of you, Pop,
> So gentle and pure,
> You make me feel safe
> Like I can endure.

When I think of you, Pop,
I think of a man
Who will always do
The best that he can.

When I think of you, Pop,
I feel so proud,
And I want to come and tell you
This truth out loud.

The next day, Hannah went back to the hospital and read her poem to her father, and he smiled when she finished.

"I'm proud of you, Pop."

She didn't know how much time she had left with him. She decided that she would come home every weekend to visit him. She longed to be with him, to spend time with him, to hold his hand. He was her Pop, her guide, and her protector. She didn't want to think of losing him, so she kept putting that thought out of her mind. She held on to two truths: that all she had was today and that she knew her Creator loved her. These were the only two things that really mattered in this world. She was discouraged, even distraught, but not destroyed.

19

Sunshine

WITH EVERYTHING SO MUCH in the air concerning her future, Hannah was holding on to the hope that God would bless her if she kept praying for a place to live. Holding that thought in her mind, the phone rang one day while she was in her bedroom at The Refuge.

"Hannah?"

"Hey, Mom."

"I have some good news."

"Really?"

"I heard about an apartment complex that caters to the disabled. You might be able to live there with a discounted rent."

"Oh, wow. Do you have the paperwork for the apartment?"

"No, but I will get it for you and mail it to you. This is good news, darling."

"I know. It's great news," said Hannah.

When Hannah received the papers in the mail, she filled them out so she could be put on the apartment's waiting list. She also talked to the apartment manager on the phone and liked her very much.

"I hope we can get you in. But people here don't leave often. It might be a while before there's an opening," said the manager.

"That's okay. I understand. I can wait," said Hannah.

She didn't realize what that statement meant. She would soon find out. Days became weeks, and weeks became months. She concentrated on living in the present. She also prayed that God would orchestrate the events so that whatever needed to happen for Hannah to get an apartment would happen. She prayed for the person whose apartment she would be taking—that the circumstances would work out so Hannah could get that specific apartment soon.

She concentrated on being a positive energy in the group home and around the people with whom she came into contact in the outpatient program. She methodically went to her outpatient group and kept busy going to the dog park, the coffee shop, and the burger restaurant. If she focused on how long she might be in the group home, she would fall into despair. All the coping skills they taught her in inpatient and outpatient treatment in the hospital led her to think otherwise. She had to be positive. There was just simply no other way to think and still survive.

Most important, though, was the time she spent in her prayer book, meditating on the verses, seeking the God she loved, and praying scripture back to Him. Through this special time with her Creator, she felt blessed and strong in her spirit.

She thought about the people in her life and how they had grown since she had known them. Torrie was very coherent and focused on going home. She had become a very close and good friend to Hannah. Sophia found out that she was not pregnant, and she was becoming a big help around the house with washing clothes and cleaning the kitchen. Daphney and Amanda were fighting less. Even more so, they were actually sharing a laugh or two at times. Daphney was sharing her cigarettes, and Amanda was less hostile about her situation at the group home.

As for her outpatient group, Colt, Sam, and Sydney were becoming very close. Hannah always saw them sitting together in the garage of the men's home. Sam stopped talking to the radio in group. Sydney was kinder and nicer to everybody. Colt just seemed to be more relaxed around people. As for Martha and Andrea, well, Hannah still didn't know them as well, but Martha seemed to participate more in group than she used to, and Andrea, sweet Andrea, was sleeping less in class.

While Hannah was living in the group home, her dad had several more visits to the hospital, due to fainting and falling. The doctors eventually placed him on hospice care because his kidneys were failing. The end was near. While she was sitting in group one day, Hannah thought about her situation. She was beginning to fall into despair and dropped her head to her chest. She heaved a deep sigh. Then her cell phone rang.

Her mom spoke seriously over the line. Hannah walked outside of her outpatient class to talk to her.

"Sweetie, Daddy is asking to see you."

"He is? Okay. I'm leaving right now."

Hannah hung up and told Ms. Jordan that she had to leave to see her dad because he was asking for her.

Ms. Jordan felt the need to give her some instruction.

"Hannah, if you really get anxious on the road, what do you do?"

"Play some music."

"And?"

"Call my mom."

"And?"

"Pull over to the side of the road," said Hannah.

"Yes, that's right. Take care of yourself. Have a safe trip."

"Okay. Thanks, Ms. Jordan."

Hannah looked over at Colt and smiled weakly. After she left the room, she noticed that Colt was following her.

"Hey, Hannah."

"Hey," she said.

"You going to be okay?"

"I hope so."

"You're stronger than you think."

"Thanks, Colt."

He walked out to her SUV with her. She turned and faced him, and for a moment, they just looked at each other. Then he pushed a curl of her hair behind her ear and smiled. She felt a tingle and a lift in her stomach from this tender gesture.

"Bye, Colt," she smiled back.

"Have a safe trip," he said.

Hannah paused for a moment, looking into Colt's eyes. Then, she got into her car and drove toward the interstate, watching him in the rearview mirror. She needed to make a stop at The Refuge to get some overnight clothes and toiletries. When she got back on the road, she was filled with a myriad of emotions—fear and sorrow about her dad, joy and excitement about Colt, and a deep vulnerability towards God—because she knew everything was in His perfect timing.

A phone call came while she was driving on the road.

"Hello," Hannah answered.

"Is this Ms. Truefield?"

"Yes."

"I think we have an apartment for you."

"Really? I can't believe it."

"It's an upstairs. Is that okay?"

"Sure, it's okay."

"Can you come by tomorrow to fill out some paperwork?"

"Absolutely. Thanks."

Hannah hung up the phone in disbelief. Again, she was dumbfounded, but this time, she tried to be hopeful. She told herself that now she would be able to stay in her hometown and spend time with her dad in his last days. No more group home. No more outpatient treatment. She was about to be free.

Like a butterfly shedding its cocoon, Hannah was letting go of the things that were keeping her from her ultimate goal of a life of independence. She knew her dad was dying, and she could feel herself grieving. Still, she felt like getting an apartment was an answer to prayer. Even in her grief, she felt the tiniest bit hopeful.

When she reached her parents' house, she walked in and found her beloved father lying in a hospital bed in their den. She walked up to him and kissed him on his bald forehead.

"Hey, Pop."

He opened his eyes. "Hey," he said.

Hannah's eyes welled up. "It's so good to see you, Daddy."

"You too."

They chatted good-naturedly about what daddies and their little girls talk about: the drive over, the weather, what ball game was on that night, and did she feel safe at the group home.

"I got an apartment, Pop."

"You did?"

"I'm moving in a month. They have to get the apartment ready."

"Okay. Good deal."

They talked for a few minutes more until her dad closed his eyes and dozed off. Hannah was so glad that she came to see him. From now on, until he left this earth, she would be near him. It was the way it was meant to be.

Hannah dug a journal out of her satchel and decided to write while her daddy slept. She began to write a very special prayer.

"Dear Father in Heaven,

"I sit here with my daddy, my dad, my Pop, the father you gave to me. I adore him. You know he means the world to me. I think about how much he means to me, and I think about how little time we have left together on this earth. All I want to do is to be near him, to watch him rest, to kiss his forehead, to hold his hand.

"Heavenly Father, You know that my dad is a good man and loves Jesus. Pop is so humble and kind, generous and sensitive, gracious and loving. I am so grateful You gave him to me. Now it's time for me to give him back to You. I know You know that this breaks my heart.

"The daddy You gave me has been my protector, my provider, my rock. Now You must become these things to me, as it should be. He modeled for me what a Father God is. A strong yet gentle hand to guide me through life. I trust You, God. You are my Protector, my Provider, my Rock. I guess You always have been. I just didn't realize it until now.

"Please don't let my daddy suffer in great pain. I long to be where he is going, to be with You. Now You are my Daddy, God. Please take good care of me—and take good care of him. In Jesus' name, amen."

After she finished writing, Hannah's cell phone rang. She saw that Colt was calling her. When Hannah answered, Colt leapt into a barrage of words, stumbling over each sentence. Hannah took her phone out on the patio away from her father's earshot.

"Colt, are you okay? I can't understand you. Speak slower."

"Hannah. I need you. I need you, Hannah."

"Colt, what is it? Are you in trouble?"

"No, I mean. . . I mean I don't need you for something specific. I mean I need you." He paused, then spoke again. "I need you, Hannah."

They both were quiet for a few seconds.

"Hannah, are you there?"

"Yes, Colt, I'm just trying to process this."

He paused. "Listen, Hannah, I need to tell you something. I don't want you to move back to your hometown. I want you to stay in Houston. I want you to be near me when I get out of outpatient. Like I said, I need you."

Hannah took a deep breath and let the air out of her chest. She thought a few seconds and closed her eyes.

"Okay, Colt, I know we talked about dating after outpatient, but I've really been thinking, and I need to tell you something."

"Okay."

"You say you need me, but I want you to need God first."

"What?"

"I need you to put God first in your life before you think about dating me," said Hannah.

"Why?" asked Colt.

"You need to know that God loves you before you can love me better."

"But. . .wait. I don't understand," said Colt.

"Okay. Let me try to explain," Hannah breathed a deep breath. "All these months that I've been in outpatient, I've really been seeking God."

"Uh huh."

"And what I've learned is how much I need Him."

Colt spoke slowly. "Okay."

"And I want you to experience the same thing."

A pause emanated over the phone. Colt finally spoke. "So. . . you think. . . God actually loves me?"

"Absolutely. He's a good father."

Colt paused a moment, then spoke again. "Okay. . . but how good?"

"Well. . . He gave His son to die for all the wrongs, or sins, you've done so you would not spend eternity without Him. He did this to show you his grace and mercy."

Colt paused. "I'm trying to understand, Hannah."

"Look, Colt, remember when we talked about God being your father and about you getting to know Him better?"

"Yeah. Sure."

"Well, I just think this is a good time to focus on that and to seek God with all your heart."

Colt paused. "Okay. . .but I don't understand what you want me to do."

Hannah paused a moment to gain her courage. Then she spoke. "Confess your sins to Jesus and thank Him for dying for you. Believe in Him—place your faith in Him. It's the only way to reach God."

Colt paused a moment. "Um. . . okay. . .but let's say I know I need God. Why Jesus, Hannah? I'm a pretty good guy. You know me."

Hannah breathed again. "God's design was to use Jesus to be the way to heaven, Colt. Just our good works can't get us to God. He's too holy, too pure for us to reach Him by ourselves. We need the purity of Jesus to get us to the Father. In the Bible, Jesus said, 'I am the way and the truth and the life. No one comes to the Father except through me.' That's in the book of John, chapter fourteen, verse six."

"So, you really want me to believe in Jesus? You want Jesus to be my God?"

"Yes. I mean, I hope so. But I want you to know that whatever you decide, I will still be your friend. But I can't date you unless we are both pursuing God. I know it sounds like I want you to follow Him for me. But, please, do it for yourself, for your soul."

They were silent for a few moments. Hannah spoke again.

"Do you. . . feel. . . kind of. . . overwhelmed?"

"Yes. I'm not sure what to think," said Colt.

"Do. . . you think. . . maybe, you could give it a try?"

"Try what?"

"Seeking God."

"How?"

"By reading scripture and praying to Him."

"And then what?"

"The Bible says, 'If you declare with your mouth "Jesus is Lord," and believe in your heart that God raised him from the dead, you will be saved.' That's from the book of Romans, chapter ten, verse nine."

Colt sighed. "And what if I can't do that?"

"God will lead you to where you need to be," said Hannah.

Colt paused. "Okay, Hannah, I will try to seek God, but I don't know how things will turn out."

"I understand. And look, I would love to live near you, but I need to be near my daddy." She paused. "He's dying, Colt."

Colt was silent on the phone again. "I'm so sorry." Then he didn't say anything for a while.

"Are you there?" Hannah finally asked.

"Yeah, I was just thinking."

"Okay."

"Well, I understand that you need to be near your father. And I understand that you want me to think about this Jesus thing. But when will we talk again?"

Again, Hannah took some time to think. "How about we give it about three months?"

"Three months? Really? That's a long time, Hannah."

"I know, but seeking God takes time. It just does."

"Wow. You're really serious about all this."

"Yes, I know. I really am. I'm coming back to The Refuge tomorrow to get my stuff and move out. I'm leaving the program. I will have an apartment down here in about a month. Until then, I will be staying with my mom and dad. I will see you tomorrow, okay? Then we can say goodbye, for now."

"I can't wait to see you, Hannah."

"Will you think about what we talked about?"

"Yes, I will," Colt said firmly. "Take care and be safe."

"Okay, thanks. Bye."

After Hannah hung up the phone, she went inside to take a shower and put her pajamas on, just like she did at The Refuge. She thought about her experience there and about her conversation with Colt. She was flooded with realizations and epiphanies that seemed to be pouring through her.

All this time she had wanted independence and autonomy, but she thought about her dad and how dependent she was on him. She thought about her mom and how much Hannah needed her. She thought about her brother and what a support he was to her. She thought of all the people she had come to know in Houston. Then she thought even bigger. She thought about God Almighty.

After thinking about all the relationships in her life that were important to her and the friends she met at The Refuge, she realized that being completely independent was impossible unless she wanted to be an island. Hannah didn't want that reality in her life. She wanted a life of community, just like the community she found in The Refuge and in the outpatient program.

She sought for the word that could define her existence at that time, and she found it—interdependent. That was the word. She could be independent but also interdependent. Sure, she could still live in an apartment as much on her own as she was able. However, she also wanted to be interdependent: with God, with others. She would strive to be independent, but she would still pursue relationships with those she loved—God first, people second. She was convinced that she was making the right choice.

Crawling into bed at her parents' home, Hannah breathed a sigh of relief. She didn't go to sleep for several hours. Those neurotransmitters were bouncing around quite rapidly in her head.

THE NEXT MORNING, she was awakened by sunlight. Hannah opened her eyes and squinted at the rays penetrating through the blinds in her bedroom. The sun was so bright, Hannah felt like it was blinding her. She blinked and tried to focus her eyes. She saw her mom standing by her bed.

"Hey, Sweetie. Your dad's awake."

Hannah's sleepy expression slowly grew into a smile that blended with the beaming sunshine lighting up her face. She threw back the covers and sat up. She was ready to close a chapter on her life and start a new one.

Humming a tune in her head, Hannah threw on some clothes, put a headband on, grabbed her duffel bag, and headed for the kitchen. She grabbed a piece of bread, smeared butter on it, and ate it in a few bites. Then she kissed her mom and dad goodbye and headed for her SUV. About twenty minutes later, she was driving on the interstate westbound to Houston. She looked in the rearview mirror and smiled. Her eyes showed a healthy gleam. She then donned her sunglasses and gunned her SUV.

She thought about her life the past year. She experienced incredible trauma only six months ago for twenty-eight days in the main hospital. She then entered a situation of uncertainty upon her discharge and became an unsure occupant of the group home. She endured the drama and made some good friends. Now she was entering into freedom like she had never known before.

Could she make it? Could she survive? All she knew was that driving down the road, Hannah felt very much alive, and she was grateful for the God who made her. He was her sustenance through her great journey of recovery from a mental breakdown. Her next journey would be dealing with her father's decline and facing life somewhat on her own while still living with a mental illness. She felt a bit overwhelmed and tried to focus on the present.

What she discovered was that deep down, she was simply content. She had peace, enough peace to help her follow the road before her and approach her journey onward with hope.

"You will seek Me and find Me when you seek Me with all your heart."   Jeremiah 29:13 (NIV)

Acknowledgements

I am very grateful to God, my Heavenly Father, for His love for me and for enabling me to write and publish this book. I am also grateful to Jesus, my Lord, my Savior, my King, my friend, for showing me what true love is.

Many good souls helped me in the process and production of this book. I am indebted to all of them. I want to thank Katy Huggins, my sister, for the creative way she designed the cover. I also want to show my appreciation to Barbara Hotz and Erin Greneaux for painstakingly editing this book. I am very grateful to the both of you.

I also want to thank all the readers who took the time to ingest this project: Mom, Katy, Russ, Pidge, and Becca. Thanks so much for reading. Also reading were Colleen Paxton, Marti Thomas, Tom and Pam Messonnier, Jodi Guillory, Susan Comeaux, Kelly Duplantis, Cheryl Evans, Carol Stubbs, and Nancy Rust. Thanks so much for giving your valuable time.

I also want to thank Carol Stubbs for her valuable editing and formatting expertise and Tom Messonnier for his consistent, gentle accountability to push me to get this thing done. I also want to show my deep appreciation to Charlene Banna for challenging me to be a better writer.

For their special encouragement, I want to thank Mark and Marti Thomas, Susan Malcolm, Lisa Delahoussaye, Jackie Hebert, Brent and Rose Bollich, Ryan and Tonya Teten, Nancy Sisley, Jodi Guillory, Karen Kulbeth, Jess Walters, Rachel Halsell, and Melissa Shannon.

About the Author:

Ann Elizabeth Yeager developed a passion for writing as a young girl. She wrote little rhymes in her poetry book and felt excited about this newfound yearning to write. In high school, her favorite class was English, where she wrote many essays, focusing mainly on the character development she discovered in novels. She graduated from the University of Southwestern Louisiana with a Bachelor of Arts degree in English. Over the years, she has loved writing sketches for dramatic presentations in her church. She has worked with her church's drama teams, both youth and adult, as a writer and director. She also worked as a journalist for a local paper, writing a movie review column and crafting articles on mental health issues. She makes her home in south Louisiana. If you are interested in reading her blog, go to www.AnnElizabethYeager.com.

About the Cover Designer:

Raised in Lafayette, Louisiana, designer and illustrator Katy Huggins moved to Texas to attend the Art Institute of Houston, where she obtained her Associates degree in Visual Communications. Huggins has worked for creative departments from small design firms to corporate in-house Marketing and Advertising Departments. Illustration has always been her forte but not always a part of her daily creative routine or "day job." Illustrating for books has been a lifelong dream of hers, ever since she first started drawing as a child every Sunday morning before church, alongside her father at the breakfast table.

This is Huggins' second published illustration work. She designed the cover of this book, and she is excited for future publication opportunities. Huggins lives in Pearland, TX with her husband and black Labrador, Lola.

Comments from Readers:

"Yeager writes with clarity and compassion, vividly describing the experience of living in a group home for people with a mental illness. The immediacy and intimacy of Hannah's story makes me feel as if I've experienced her world and the challenges of recovering from mental illness. *Holding on to a Sound Mind* will leave you with a greater compassion for the human condition and a greater faith in human nature… and in God."

- Marti Thomas, *Executive Pastor*

"This is a story of hope. It's a story about living with mental illness and how that affects relationships and plans for the future. Hannah's journey is one of courage, strength and determination as she learns to take control of her life and illness."

- Carol Stubbs, *Author*

"Through this humble story of an individual's season of life, Yeager takes you through both the struggles and the hope that can be found in living with mental illness. This personal and entertaining story will tug at your heart while being eye-opening and informative, giving you a better understanding of what it's like to deal with mental illness."

- Jodi Guillory, *Creative Director*